better late than staked

Vella Day

Erotic Reads Publishing

A Voodoo and Vampire Mystery
A Witch's Cove Whodunit
Book 2

www.velladay.com

velladayauthor@gmail.com

Cover Art by Jaycee DeLorenzo

Edited by Rebecca Cartee

Published in the United States of America

E-book ISBN: 978-1-951430-50-4

Print book ISBN: 978-1-951430-51-1

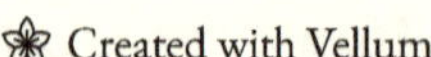

about the book

A cold case, a ghost in need of something to do, and a freshly dead victim of a vampire slaying. Now that's right up my alley.

Hi, I'm Rihanna Samuels, a nineteen year old mind reader, from Witch's Cove, Florida. When the ghost of the woman who was killed on a cruise ship last month asks for my help to solve the cold case of a hit-and-run in Nebraska, what could I say?

What anyone would: no! That is until she looked so dejected that I had to find out more about the person she wanted me to help. The case wasn't all that interesting, but hey, I was on spring break, and I thought I could convince my boyfriend to help.

Here's the rub. We didn't end up with the case we started out to solve. Nope. We found another dead body that I feared was the result of a vampire attack. That's when I knew we needed help from our old friend, Lorenzo Bambini III. Sure, he's a ghost, too, but I was convinced he was the key to solving our case.

chapter one

"PSST. RIHANNA. I NEED YOUR HELP."

I jerked up from looking through the camera photos I'd taken yesterday and blinked. "Bella Benoit? What are you doing here?"

My former cruise ship roommate smiled and floated over to the end of my bed. And by floated, I meant her rather translucent being moved toward me. And yes, she is a ghost—one I hadn't seen in weeks.

"Yup. That's me. I haven't aged a day, have I?" The teenager actually spun around and laughed, a sound that was rather foreign, since the last time I'd seen her was to help solve her murder.

"No, you look the same." She even had that voodoo doll in her hand. In fact, she was wearing the same nightwear she had on when she was murdered. "I'm surprised to see you, that's all."

She dipped her head. "You mean because I didn't say goodbye when the cruise was over?"

"Yes. I kind of put my own life in danger to help you, and when we solved your murder, you and Lorenzo left without so much as a thank you." Wow. I hadn't realized how angry I was about the whole thing.

"I'm sorry. It's just that I really wanted to see if I could connect with my dad."

I doubted a person with no magic could see a ghost, but it was awesome that she wanted to try. "And did you?"

"Kind of. He realized I was there, but he couldn't hear me —at least at first."

"At first?" I asked.

"I kind of cheated. I asked my grandmother to act as an interpreter since she could interact with me."

"Cool." That was what I had offered to do, but it made more sense for her voodoo high priestess grandmother to be the intermediary instead. "With your grandmother present, could your father hear you?"

"On and off. And when he could, he cried." She shrugged. "He was quite upset about my death and kept telling me it was his fault for sending me on the cruise."

Why did people always blame themselves for things they had no control over? "I doubt your father understood the dynamics on the boat. If anything, the captain was to blame for making the change in room assignments." Though the killer was the real guilty party.

"I guess." She sighed. "But that's water under the bridge as you once told me."

"I did. By the way, where is Lorenzo?" The fellow vampire ghost had been her constant companion.

"I don't know. I saw him once in New Orleans, but he was really distracted. I went to find him again, but he was gone."

"That's too bad." I liked Lorenzo. For being dead, he had a great attitude.

In case anyone was wondering who I am and how I met Bella, my name is Rihanna Samuels. Like Bella, I'm nineteen years old, but that's kind of where the similarities stop.

Thanks to a connection from college, I landed a six-day photo assignment aboard a fifty-five passenger yacht cruise to Mexico. I was incredibly excited until I met my tattooed and pierced roommate. Bella was a piece of work, but I later learned there were reasons for her bad attitude. The sad part was that she was murdered the next day.

As she mentioned, Bella wouldn't have even been on the boat, except that her dad told her she needed to get a job. In reality, he was trying to keep her from being harmed by some wacky bank client. Too bad he didn't let her in on that secret, not that he could have prevented her death.

Bella was sitting at the end of my bed like she used to do on the boat, when there was a light knock on the door to my room. It opened just a bit so my cousin, Glinda Goodall, could stick her head in. My bedroom was in the back of her office, and she often stopped in to say hi.

She looked around. "Are you okay? I heard you talking to someone."

I wasn't sure why that would be strange. I could have been video chatting with my boyfriend or speaking with him on the phone. "I'm good. Actually, Bella Benoit just showed up needing my help."

Her brows rose. "Oh?"

Even though Glinda was a witch, she couldn't see or hear Bella, which was rather strange as she often interacted with ghosts. Only my cousin's nine-pound, pink iguana familiar could see and hear her.

Speaking of the little trouble maker, Iggy waddled in. He came over to the bed and looked up. "Is that Bella?" He'd spoken to Bella during one of my video chats with Glinda.

She smiled. "It sure is. It's cool to see you in person, Mr. Iggy. You are so dang cute."

Iggy looked over at me. If he could have planted his claws

on his hips, he would have. Being called cute wasn't something he liked. "Whatcha doing here?" he asked her.

"I met a lady in the afterlife who had been murdered, and she asked me to help her figure out who did it since the sheriff in her hometown seems to have dropped the ball. You might remember us talking about her. Her name is Lara Finley."

"The woman who was in the hit and run accident in Nebraska?" he asked.

Wow. I was really impressed that Iggy remembered that. Usually, only things important to him stuck in his brain.

"Yes."

"Does Lara have any idea who ran her off the road?" I didn't remember many details when I'd spoken with Lara's brother. At the time, I was trying to solve Bella's murder.

"No. She thinks she must have hit her head, because she kind of lost her memory regarding the few days leading up to the accident." Bella leaned forward. "I didn't have the heart to tell her that from the way she looked, she hit more than just her head, because ghosts don't like to know that stuff."

I chuckled. "Good to know."

Since Glinda could only hear my half of the conversation, Iggy quietly told my cousin what Bella said.

"What do you think I can do?" I asked.

"I was hoping you'd investigate," Bella said.

I blew out a breath. "Bella, that is sweet of you to want to help her, but I have classes to attend." Actually, I was on spring break, but I had planned to spend time with my boyfriend, who was also on his break from college. "Besides, I'm not any kind of sleuth. Glinda and Jaxson are."

"Oh." Bella looked over at Glinda and waved. No surprise, Glinda didn't respond. Bella sighed. "How can your cousin help me, if she can't see or hear me?"

"That could be a problem, but remember, I'm just a photographer." So what if I'd helped Glinda solve numerous cases as well as solved Bella's murder? When she started to float away, guilt filled me. "Wait."

Bella turned around and smiled. "You changed your mind?"

It stunk that I couldn't read a ghost's thoughts, but I had the sense I'd just been played. "Possibly. Tell me more about what Lara said about the car wreck. She must have seen something."

"Not much. Just that some bright lights had raced up behind her right before the car rammed into her rear bumper and kept pushing her until she went down the embankment and into a tree."

"How horrible. I know the accident happened in Nebraska, but was it on a country road where there wasn't much traffic?"

Bella nodded. "And it was at night."

"Who found her?"

"She doesn't know. She was dead."

"Bella," Glinda said. "Iggy just said that you told Rihanna that this dead woman doesn't know who found her. As a ghost, how long was it before you became aware of what was going on in the world?"

"Rihanna, you and your family always ask such hard questions. Tell her that it was a while. As soon as I realized I was dead, I came back to our cabin, but you would know better. When did I show up?"

I had to think. "Maybe twelve hours after you died?"

"Yikes."

"Rihanna," Glinda said. "Since Gavin is free, maybe the two of you could use this as a vacation together. You know him. Gavin will probably spend most of his break at his mother's morgue anyway. He is totally focused on his medical career."

She had a point. Gavin wanted to be a doctor more than

anything. "I'll ask him, but I'm not all that hopeful he'll say yes."

Bella clapped, but as was the case with ghosts, her hands went right through each other. I couldn't imagine how tough it must be to have lost so much.

"You'll come with me then?" Bella asked as she returned to the edge of my bed.

"How about if I let you know tomorrow?" I needed time to think about it. "If I do go, it will cost money since I'll need a plane ticket and a place to stay. You'll have to understand that I can't be there for more than this week as I have school."

Bella smiled. "That's okay. I told Lara that I'd convince you to help. I don't think she expects you to be successful."

That wasn't very encouraging. "Nice to know." I placed the camera I had been holding on the bed. "If you were with your dad in New Orleans, how did you run into Lara? And how did you even know who she was?" I was quite sure they hadn't met when they were alive.

Bella laughed. "It's not like you die in Nebraska and then float above it for the rest of your life."

That made sense. "Does this mean you've crossed over?"

She tucked in her chin. "No! I'm not eager to find out what's in store for me. Knowing my life, I'd be sent to a place I don't want to go."

I didn't think those into voodoo believed in the conventional Heaven and Hell, but what did I know? "Okay, but how did Lara find you? Was she aware that you were on the same cruise ship as her brother?"

Bella lifted off of my bed and floated around—her version of pacing. "I think I was complaining that I had been murdered, and Lara overheard me. I can be a little loud, you know."

I swallowed a laugh. "I do know that. Then what happened?"

"I recognized her name."

I probably would never understand how these two met, but I supposed it didn't matter. "You told her you'd help by asking me to take the case, right?"

"Yes."

It had been quite the adventure trying to find Bella's killer. "I see. Stop by tomorrow, and I'll let you know."

"Okay." As quickly as she arrived, Bella left.

I blew out a breath. "What do you think?" I asked Glinda.

Thankfully, Iggy had translated everything to her. "You should do it," Iggy said.

I was speaking to my cousin. "Thank you, Iggy. Glinda, any words of advice?"

"I trust you, but you know that you can always ask our two gargoyle shifters to help," she said.

Genevieve and Hugo could teleport anywhere in seconds. Hugo, in particular, had many abilities to stop a person from harming me should the situation arise. "I know, and I appreciate that." I slipped off the bed. "I need to discuss this with Gavin. I know he was anxious to learn what he could from his mom during his short break. He might not want to spend time away from the morgue."

Glinda nodded. "I understand, but if anyone can convince him, it's you."

"I hope so."

I thought about calling him, but Gavin might be in the middle of an autopsy. Besides, asking him in person would be better. I grabbed a light sweater and left the office that was situated above Jaxson's brother's wine and cheese shop. The wind whipped off the ocean, scenting the air with a deliciously salty bouquet. From the frequent temperature changes we'd been experiencing during the day, spring would be here before we knew it, and with it would come very warm weather.

The walk to the morgue would take less than five minutes,

which would give me time to decide if I even wanted to help Bella—or rather Lara Finley—a woman I'd never met.

I loved taking photos. The creative process soothed my soul, but trying to figure people out and helping others might be an even bigger high.

At the moment, I wasn't planning on following in Glinda's footsteps, but seeking the truth was in my blood. My dad had been an undercover FBI agent, and part of what he did appealed to me. Right now, though, I needed to see if Gavin would go with me. I certainly couldn't count on Bella doing much, other than spying on people, and I didn't like asking Genevieve and Hugo to be there on the off chance I needed saving. That wasn't my style.

When I arrived at the morgue, I stepped inside. Since it wasn't a place that people visited, there wasn't a receptionist. I knocked on the morgue door in the hopes Gavin was inside.

A voice came over the speaker. "May I help you?"

"Hey, Elissa. It's me, Rihanna. I'm looking for Gavin."

"He's here. I'll send him out."

"Thanks."

It would take him a while to wash up before coming out. While I waited, I braced myself for all of his objections. Not only would Gavin say it wasn't safe to hunt down a killer—and he'd be right—but he'd correctly note that he couldn't help if he couldn't see or hear a ghost.

Ugh. Solve both of those issues, and we might be on a plane to Nebraska tomorrow.

chapter two

THE DOOR to the morgue opened, and my handsome boyfriend emerged. Gavin was drying his hands—hands that would carry the stench of death on them for a while. Thankfully, I was pretty used to the smell.

He stepped over and lightly kissed me. "What's up?"

I inhaled. "No dead body?"

He shook his head. "No one needed an autopsy today. So as not to delay my education, Mom purchased a heart and was showing me how to autopsy it."

How fun. Not. "That's nice of her."

"It was, so to what do I owe the pleasure?"

"It's complicated."

Gavin grinned, and I kind of swooned. "Try me."

I patted the seat next to me, and he sat down. "Remember, I told you how my roommate on the boat was murdered, and that she came back as a ghost?"

"Yes, and then some vampire ghost showed up, and the three of you—with the help of some of our Witch's Cove friends—solved the murder case."

I smiled. "Good memory. Yes. Well, Bella showed up today in my room."

He dipped his chin. "What did she want?"

I explained about Lara Finley's death and her plea to help Bella solve her murder. "I thought, maybe, I'd see what I could find out."

"Via the Internet? Or would you actually go to Nebraska?"

He didn't have to sound so surprised—or maybe his tone implied he didn't approve. And yes, I could have read his mind, but I didn't like doing so unless I had to. "We'd have to fly to Nebraska. Since we're both on spring break, I have the time."

"We?"

I rubbed his arm and gave him my best pout. "I was hoping you'd come with me."

He chuckled. "To Nebraska?" I nodded. "Dare I ask if the town is near Omaha?"

"I haven't looked where Netwood is located, but with my luck, it will be in the middle of nowhere." I didn't know why he'd care. This wasn't a sightseeing trip.

"You do realize it will be cold there at this time of year?"

I hadn't thought of that. "Only kind of cold, right? It will be spring soon."

"Let's hope. How about we grab a bite to eat, and we can discuss this?"

"You are the best."

"I haven't said I'll go with you, but you know I can't let you run off by yourself."

"I was hoping you'd say that. Besides, if you don't go with me, we won't be able to see each other at all during our break."

"Maybe you should switch majors and become a lawyer."

I laughed. I could be quite convincing when needed.

The closest eating place was The Spellbound Diner, run by one of the best gossip queens in all of Witch's Cove, Dolly

Andrews. Unfortunately, she wouldn't be able to help us with this case.

We found a vacant booth, and as soon as we slipped in, someone other than Dolly came over and took our order. Since I ate at the diner a lot—and I mean a lot—I knew what I wanted, and apparently, so did Gavin.

"Tell me what you know about this case," he said.

I loved that he sounded so analytical. It was almost as if he was asking a nurse about a patient's symptoms.

"Not much other than Lara was run off the road at night and died. Obviously, the killer fled the scene, or we'd know who it was. Lara doesn't seem to believe much progress has been made in her case, though it's possible she might not be in the know since she is deceased."

"Why again do you want to fly to a possibly cold climate for a week and put yourself in the crosshairs of a killer?" he asked.

"I don't know, but I have the urge to help." I let out a deep breath. "It's not that I'm bored at school, but I feel as if I've moved on. My classes aren't really motivating me anymore. Does that make sense?"

He smiled. "I was wondering when you'd realize you are a better photographer than probably half the staff at your college."

Gavin was just saying that to make me feel better. "I don't know about that, but I want more than just to capture other people's joys and sorrows." I leaned forward. "I was alive when I was helping Bella. It's different when I'm in charge than when I'm following Glinda around."

Gavin reached over and clasped my hand. "Then I say we should go to Nebraska to explore this need of yours."

I grinned. "Thank you. I knew I picked the right guy."

He chuckled. "There is the problem of me not seeing or hearing your ghost friend. I know Glinda put a spell on Jaxson and Steve so that they could hear familiars, but what about ghosts?"

"That is an issue. Even Glinda can't see Bella. Only Iggy can. I will admit needing to translate everything is a pain and sometimes impractical."

"Didn't you say that Hugo was able to help Jaxson's parents hear their familiar talk?"

"He did," I said. "But remember, Bella isn't a familiar."

He shrugged. "What about Gertrude or Levy? Maybe they can help."

"That's a brilliant idea." Gertrude Poole was a very old psychic from Witch's Cove who was great at contacting the dead. "I'm not sure Gertrude is the best at spells, but her grandson might be. Let me ask him." I pulled out my phone and called Levy Poole.

He answered on the third ring. "Rihanna! This is a surprise."

Usually, my cousin was the one who contacted the head of the local coven. "I know, but I have a dilemma."

"I love challenges. Do tell."

As quickly as I could, I outlined what happened on my cruise, and how the ghost of the dead girl had returned. "She wants me to help her solve another crime. In Nebraska."

"How can I help?"

I was hoping he'd ask. "I want Gavin to come with me, but he can't see or hear Bella. Do you know of a spell to enable him to see ghosts?"

One time, Glinda had swallowed a potion to turn Iggy from pink to green, and while she failed at that mission, it enabled her to see ghosts—at least most of the time. The difference here was that Glinda was a witch, and Gavin possessed no powers.

"That's a tough one. If you two want to stop over at the library in an hour, I can see if we can figure something out. It just so happens, a woman who is a master of spells, is in a town."

My pulse soared. "We'll be there. All I want is a chance."

Levy chuckled. "See you soon."

I disconnected and turned to Gavin. "Good news. It's possible that Levy can figure something out. He asked us to meet him at the library in an hour."

"You mean at his *secret* coven back room?"

Gavin had been paying attention. "Yes."

I was unsure if this would work, but Levy and his coven were my best hope at performing this miracle. As we followed Levy down the long hallway to the back room of the library, Gavin seemed fascinated by the pictures on the walls.

"Ordinary people don't come back here, right?" he asked.

"No, they don't. Few people ever have had the chance to see the coven's secret meeting space. Just wait until you see the books Levy's coven has. Not only are they old, some of the books contain some really strange spells and stuff."

Inside their inner sanctum, two people were seated around a large table. The woman, who was about sixty, must have been the visiting spell master. She had on a red business suit, adorned with a beautiful onyx necklace, and her hair was pulled back into some kind of intricate braid.

"Hi," I said.

She smiled. "Hello, I'm Melissa. Nice to meet you." She shook our hands.

"Like I mentioned on the phone, she is our spell master," Levy announced.

I had no idea a spell master even existed. "I'm Rihanna Samuels, and this is my boyfriend, Gavin Sanchez."

The other gentleman stood and shook our hands. "I'm Wes. I'm here to help Melissa, or rather watch her do her magic. I'm really just an apprentice."

"Cool." I'm sure Glinda would have liked to have Melissa as a mentor.

Levy motioned we take a seat. Why I was nervous I didn't know. I could already see ghosts. Boy, could I.

Levy nodded to Melissa to begin.

"I've only performed this spell one time on a non-magical person who claimed he was able to see ghosts afterward, but no one could confirm it."

That wasn't encouraging. "I wish I could contact *my ghost* as I call her. That way, we could give Gavin a test."

As if Bella had been in the room all along, she suddenly appeared. The fact everyone's eyes widened, implied they, too, could see her.

"Hi, everyone." Bella spun around.

Wasn't she chipper? "Gavin, Bella is here, so we'll be able to see if the spell works."

"She's in the room?" Everyone nodded. "Hi, Bella, wherever you are. I'm Gavin."

"Oh, Rhianna, you didn't tell me he was so hot."

I chuckled. "He is indeed. Did you hear that Melissa is going to put a spell on Gavin in the hopes he can see and hear you?"

"Yes. I'm really excited. What would you like me to do?"

I figured Melissa would be better at answering that question, so I nodded at her.

"Bella, if you would move behind Gavin for now, that would be great. I want your energy to be near him, but I don't want you to distract him too much."

Bella smiled. "Okay."

She nodded at Levy, who pressed a button that dimmed the overhead lights. I had no idea what she had placed in the bowl in front of her, but when the contents caught fire, even I was surprised. I hadn't seen her light anything. Then again, it was magic.

Gavin reached over and clasped my hand. It wasn't from fear, but rather I sensed interest and excitement. I was especially happy that Bella didn't make one of her usual snarky comments.

Melissa began to chant in some ancient sounding language. The lights flickered, dimmed, and then brightened somewhat. It was possible that Levy or Wes was doing something to them to make the spell seem more authentic, or else Melissa was the real deal.

Red smoke rose up from the bowl and floated into the room.

"It's done," Melissa said. Immediately, the lights brightened. She looked over at Bella. "Would you come here, please?"

Bella glanced my way and then did as Melissa asked.

Gavin pushed back his chair and stood. "What is that?"

"What is what?" I wanted to be certain he was talking about Bella's ghost.

When he pointed to Bella, my heart raced. "That."

"He sees me?" Bella grinned.

Gavin stilled. "Is she real?"

Did he think I would play a joke on him? "Yes, that's Bella. The spell worked!"

Probably to impress him, Bella spun in a circle. "This is cool. Rihanna, now you and Gavin can fly to Nebraska and help solve Lara's murder."

"I can't believe it." Gavin was a scientist, and as such, I had the sense he'd been merely humoring Glinda and me by pretending to believe that Iggy could communicate with us, but I didn't think he truly believed in it. Even after the spell, I doubted he would be able to hear Iggy. But would his ability to see Bella change his mind about the occult in general?

"By any chance does Gavin's new supernatural ability extend to familiars?" I asked Melissa.

"It could."

That would be so great. "I can't thank you all enough."

"Go ahead and pay them, Rihanna," Bella said.

Before I could answer, Levy held up his hand. "We don't take payment. We like helping people."

"Wow." Bella sounded quite impressed.

I pushed back my chair and stood. "Again, thank you." I turned to Gavin. "Ready to book our flight?"

"I guess so, but what about Bella? She won't be on the plane with us, will she?" he whispered.

"I think not." I turned back to my ghost friend. "Bella, stop by the office tonight, and we'll tell you when we plan to arrive in Netwood and which hotel we'll be staying at. We'll meet you in Nebraska."

She did a mock salute. "Ay, ay, captain."

"Funny."

Bella disappeared. After I said goodbye to the coven members, I led Gavin back down the hallway. Once outside, he faced me. "Did I really see a ghost, or was that some mechanical device?"

I hugged him. "Trust me. Bella is the real deal. I'm hoping you won't regret that you can now see and hear her. Sometimes I wish I couldn't."

Gavin dragged a hand down his chin. I didn't need to be a mind reader to know he was having a hard time dealing with this issue.

"I know Glinda is a witch and that she has a talking pink iguana. I might have thought she was crazy, except that you can hear Iggy, and then Jaxson and Steve could, too, but ghosts?"

I threaded my arm through his. "It is a bit much. I know that when I learned vampires existed, I was taken aback. I'm still not sure how much is real, except that Lorenzo Bambini is one."

"Maybe someone just stabbed him in the chest with a stake, and he's pretending to be a vampire."

Poor Gavin. I needed to be patient with him. "Maybe."

He leaned over and kissed me on the cheek. "Okay. I just need to accept this as real. Let's make those reservations."

I smiled. I had the best boyfriend in the world.

chapter three

"HOW DO WE CONTACT BELLA?" Gavin asked as he placed our suitcases next to our hotel beds.

"Excellent question. She knows that we were to arrive at the Omaha airport at seven and hoped to make it to the hotel by ten this evening."

He looked at his watch. "Since it's a little after that now, I bet she'll wait until tomorrow morning to bring us up to speed on the murder case."

That wasn't Bella's style. She didn't seem to care about time. "Perhaps."

No sooner had I sat down, than our overly anxious ghost showed up. "You made it!"

"We did."

She floated between us. "Okay, I need to catch you two up." Bella spoke very fast. "Lara is very excited that you guys are here, in part because it's quite frustrating that we can't ask questions. Like I said, the sheriff investigated her death, but he's closed the case."

"Really?" Netwood looked to be a town about the same size as Witch's Cove, which meant he probably wasn't overloaded with other murders. "Why?"

"I don't know. It's not like I can ask him," she said.

"True, so where do we start?" I asked.

"Lara suggests you speak with her husband, James."

I looked over at Gavin who faced her. "Is Lara certain that her husband didn't run her off the road?" he asked.

"I don't think she knows for sure."

I blew out a breath. "Bella, since we are only here for a few days, you need to gather as much information as possible."

"I've tried. Lara and I have talked a lot, but she wasn't all that open at first. I guess she thought I was too young, but come on. We're both dead, so does it really matter? I mean, it wasn't like I could tell many people about her secrets."

"Secrets?" I asked.

"Yeah. I finally got her to admit that her marriage was not going well. It was why she'd booked the Valentine's Day cruise to Mexico."

That had potential. "So she thinks her husband might have run her off the road?" This was becoming rather confusing.

"That's the problem. She doesn't know. The last thing she remembers is packing to go on the cruise."

I wish we'd known how difficult this was going to be before we showed up. "I thought you said she remembers seeing lights come up behind her car and then the car pushing her off the road?"

Bella waved a hand. "I meant before that."

Uh-huh.

"Bella, did Lara say why her marriage wasn't going well?" Gavin asked. "Was it because her husband worked too much, they had poor communication, or was he unfaithful?"

Bella paced. "Lara was unclear about those kind of details, but she eventually admitted that she spent a lot of time with a lawyer by the name of Daniel Weintraub."

That might have been an issue. "Was she with this Daniel guy for legal advice, or was he her lover?"

"Yeah, that."

"Her lover?" Bella nodded. Since I never was good at remembering names, I pulled out my phone and noted the man's name. "We should speak with him tomorrow."

"Rihanna," Gavin said. "We have to tread lightly. He could sue us for slander if we accuse him of anything."

"You're right. Maybe we can ask Lara to spy on him."

Gavin's eyebrows rose. "Do you think he'd just blab to a coworker that he ran her off the road? Even if he went out with friends that night, and has an ironclad alibi, he probably won't tell us anything."

I looked over at Bella. "What do you think?"

"Lara wants to feel useful, so she might agree to watch James. If Daniel killed her, I know she'd be devastated. That means I should watch Daniel, and she can check on her husband."

"I like that plan. Tomorrow, Gavin and I will visit the sheriff."

"Rihanna, we can't just waltz in and ask about an ongoing investigation. The sheriff won't tell us anything—and he shouldn't. The case isn't closed yet," Gavin said.

"Lara said it was, though she might not have her facts straight." I blew out a frustrating breath. "In that case, we should pretend we're back in Witch's Cove and find a restaurant near the sheriff's office. Someone should know something."

He smiled. "That's my girl, but who's to say the gossip tree is as prevalent here as it is in Witch's Cove?"

I smiled sweetly at him. "We won't know until we try."

Gavin huffed out a laugh. "I forgot how optimistic you are."

"That's all Glinda's doing."

"Besides checking out Lara's boyfriend—if I can call him that—what else should I do?" Bella asked.

That was a good question. "You won't be able to do much tonight, but tomorrow, find out who Lara's friends are. One of them might be willing to speak with us about her death. Gavin and I can then make contact."

She smiled. "Can do."

"Oh, before you go, ask Lara where her brother, Mr. Hackett, lives. I bet he would know something."

"You got it." And then she was gone.

Gavin dropped back onto the bed. "My mind is officially blown."

"Solving a crime is hard."

He sat up. "No. That's not it. As a future doctor, I'll be required to figure things out every day. I love that part. It's the ghost concept that is still creeping me out. Did Levy or Melissa say how long this spell would last?"

"No, probably because they might not know. The good thing is that at least you know I'm not crazy when I mention I can talk with animals and see ghosts."

He leaned over and kissed me. "I never thought you were anything but super smart and amazingly awesome."

My heart melted.

The next morning, the clerk at the hotel's front desk was very helpful in showing us where to go on a map of the town. He also recommended where we could find some good food.

Lucky for us, the sheriff's office in Netwood would be easy to find, mostly because the town was laid out in a grid pattern, three streets wide and two streets long. As luck would have it, across the street from the office was the Hillside Diner. Perfect.

It was chilly outside—okay, it was freezing by Florida standards—but I had come prepared with a warm jacket, knit hat, boots, and gloves. We'd rented a car at the airport, since Netwood was pretty far from civilization, but when in town, we decided it would be best to walk.

The one thing I could say in support of Netwood was that it was really pretty. Hills bordered the town on one end with vast fields surrounding the other three sides.

Not that it would give me much of a clue, but I wanted to locate the accident site. I supposed Lara could tell us where she died—or so I hoped.

"Ready for some chow and a little gossip?" I asked Gavin.

"You bet." He looked around. "Where's our friend?"

"I don't think Bella thinks in terms of time. She'll show up when she wants to. This trip might end up as just a fun adventure for us if Bella becomes bored with the case."

Gavin wrapped a comforting arm around my waist. "As long as we're with each other, I'm happy."

I smiled. "I hope you feel the same way in a few days if we have to spend our time investigating."

He tapped my nose and smiled as we entered the diner. Half of the ten booths were empty, so we snagged one. Beautiful paintings and photos depicting sand dunes and towering rock formations adorned the walls. The scenes were quite majestic looking.

Gavin studied the images. "Too bad we don't have more time here. If all of these places are in Nebraska, I would have liked to check them out."

"Me too."

Our server came by and handed us a menu. "Coffee for you both?"

"Sure," we said in unison.

As she poured our drinks, I decided this woman, whose name tag read Stella, looked to be in her mid-forties. That meant she might have known Lara. "We just came into town to console a man who lost his wife. Did you know Lara Finley by any chance?"

I hoped she didn't question us on how we knew James Finley, because we'd never met the man.

The waitress planted a hand on her chest. "Oh, my yes. Mrs. Finley was so sweet. It was a shame what happened to her."

"I know. It was so tragic. Murdered at such a young age."

Stella's eyes widened. "Murdered? Did James tell you that?"

Uh-oh. Caught.

"He doesn't know what happened exactly," Gavin said.

If I could communicate telepathically like our gargoyle shifter friends could, I would have congratulated Gavin on the nice save.

"I wasn't totally shocked when I heard Lara had been in an accident since she had been acting rather strangely the week before she passed. I assumed she became distracted and drove off the road and crashed."

That comment had a lot of possibilities. "What was she distracted about?"

"I don't know. She and I weren't that close, but people talk, you know."

"I do. Well, thank you." I wanted to ask more about the distraction, but I figured we might have learned all we could from Stella at the moment. I found that asking too many questions at once could actually hinder our investigation. Small towns protected their own. Besides, we could always return and speak with her again.

She smiled. "I'll be back to take your order." With that she left.

"What do you think?" I asked.

"Me? I'm just a wannabe doctor. You're the sleuth."

I chuckled. "You're confusing me with Glinda."

"Hardly. Your logical side is superior to Glinda's, though admittedly she is a better witch."

"I agree. Wannabe sleuth or not, we need Bella to find out who Lara's good friends were. They should know if she was having emotional difficulties. It's possible Lara was distracted and only thought someone pushed her off the road."

"I would think a person would know how they died, but in any case, we need to speak with the husband. I'm curious why he thinks his wife wasn't murdered," Gavin said.

"That would be good to know." I was surprised my overly protective boyfriend was willing to speak with a man who could have harmed his wife yet wanted to avoid Lara's supposed boyfriend, who might also be guilty. "Maybe we can speak with James at his workplace, wherever that is."

"Good idea. It will be safer there. Lara should be able to tell us its location, assuming ghosts can remember things like phone numbers and addresses."

I adored this man. "Bella knew her dad's number."

"Good to know."

Before Stella returned, we quickly looked over the menu. Since everything looked great, I figured I couldn't go wrong with my choice. Stella returned and took our order, but her lack of eye contact told me something was amiss. Too bad I couldn't figure out what it was. So much for being a mind reader.

A few moments later, a different server carried over our food, and Gavin and I ate in companionable silence. The whole time I worked on what our next move should be.

When we finished, we paid our bill. As soon as we stepped outside, a blast of cold, damp air assaulted us. "I miss Florida."

He smiled. "You and me both, but we are here to help both Bella and Lara, not to have a vacation."

"I know. Before we try to pick the sheriff's brain, we need

to find Bella." As we crossed the street, I pretended I was speaking with Gavin. "Bella, are you around? We need to talk with you." When she didn't appear, I grunted. "This is harder than I thought."

"We'll figure it out."

I hoped so. We walked back to the hotel, hoping Bella would find us there. She seemed to have this sixth sense about our location. I should ask her about whether or not she possessed the ability to find people in general. It was possible she merely zipped from place to place until she saw us.

We weren't back more than ten minutes when Bella showed up, and she wasn't alone.

"Are you Lara?" I couldn't imagine it being anyone else.

"Yes, that's me. I just had to meet you both. Bella has been telling me how great you both are."

Great? That was a stretch. Even after I helped figure out who'd killed Bella, I wasn't sure she liked me. Her distaste for life made for a troubled person. "Thank you. I'm glad we are finally able to meet."

"How can I help? Bella said you had a plan."

I did, but how did Bella know it?

I explained what the waitress, Stella, had said. "We thought we'd speak with your husband to get his side of the story."

She nodded. "That would be good since I don't remember being distracted. Though I could have been. I've been watching James, but I honestly can't even tell if he's upset that I'm gone."

That wasn't good. "Do you think he had something to do with your death?"

chapter four

LARA FLOATED BACK and forth across the room. It was like watching a shark that needed to move to breathe. Thankfully, Bella was sitting still.

"I hope my husband had nothing to do with my death, but I can't be sure. All I remember is him acting really odd." Lara held up a wispy hand. "And no, I don't recall why he was acting that way, or what he was doing that seemed off."

That was too bad. Hopefully, someone could help us. "Before we continue, can you tell us where your husband works and his phone number? We'd like to speak with him in a safe place," I said.

Lara looked over at Bella. "You're right. She is smart." Lara turned back to us. "He works for a financial consulting firm." She gave us the name, as well as his phone number, which I immediately put into my phone.

"Lara," Gavin said. "What was the last thing you remember?"

"Before the crash, I remember packing for the cruise to Mexico, which Bella tells me I never made."

"No, you didn't. I'm sorry. What else?" he asked.

"My father-in-law passed away in January of this year, and

I remember needing to help James clean out his home." She looked up. "I don't know why that memory jumped out at me just now, but I think it might be important."

"He lived here in Netwood, I take it?" I asked.

"Yes, but his death affected James a lot. Maybe that's why my husband was acting different."

Now we were getting somewhere. "How was he acting? Was he depressed, angry, distant, or what?"

"I'd have to say secretive. Sure, he was sad, but I expected that. James would stay late after work and make up some reason why he couldn't be home for dinner most nights. I always figured he wanted to lose himself in his work so he wouldn't have to think about his dad's passing."

"Was he meeting with clients?" If he was, it would be easy for him to prove.

"I don't know. He wouldn't talk about it, but I recall bits and pieces of our conversation. He told me not to say anything about it."

That was odd. "Say anything about what? His work habits or something else?"

Lara shook her head. "I can't remember, and trust me I have been trying to sort through everything since I died. It wasn't until I met Bella that I had any hope of figuring this out."

"Would you have confided in someone about your husband's behavior?" Gavin asked.

Lara dragged her fingers through her hair, but I doubted she achieved the affect she was looking for. "I might have, but I don't recall."

I couldn't imagine losing my memory. Though from the looks of the cuts, bruises, and blood on her face, the trauma from the accident had been extensive.

"Can you tell us the names of your closest friends? I'm thinking they might know something," I said.

"Sure." This time Gavin took down the information. Lara listed her friends in order of who she most likely would have confided in. "Oh wait. I get my nails done at a local salon, and I often chat with Becca. She doesn't say much, but she's a good listener. I can't imagine telling her anything important, though, but maybe I did."

If we interviewed all these people, it would take quite a long time. "What about your lawyer friend?"

Lara glanced over at Bella. "I see nothing is sacred."

"It's not when we are looking into your murder," Bella said, sounding quite defensive.

"I get it. What would you like to know about Daniel?"

"Could he have been responsible for your death?" I asked.

Lara stopped moving and floated onto the end of the bed. She acted a lot like Bella in that respect. "Maybe? I mean James was upset with me about something, so I told Daniel that he and I needed to take a break in order to help me figure out what I wanted to do. It was Daniel who suggested James and I go on this romantic cruise. If at the end of our trip, I wanted to stay married to James, Daniel and I would split up. If not, I would ask James for a divorce."

"That was nice of him. What about your brother?" I asked. "He took your place on the cruise."

"What about him?"

"He was very upset about your death," I said. "It seemed as if you two were close."

"Yes. Oh, my goodness. I don't know why I didn't think of Cameron. Did I tell him my deepest, darkest secrets? No, but I probably mentioned that James wasn't himself."

"Where does Cameron live?" It seemed strange to call Mr. Hackett by his first name.

"One town over, in Elkwood. He's a podiatrist."

I wasn't surprised he was a doctor. The man had sounded rather educated. "How can we contact him?"

She told us. "Thanks. Did Bella mention she was going to watch over Daniel to see if he mentioned anything about your death?"

"Yes. In fact, after I spied on James for a bit, I wanted to see Daniel. Turns out he, too, acted as if I never existed, though he does have a heavy case load. I keep telling myself that he is throwing himself into work to keep from thinking about me."

I hoped that was true, though that was what she thought about her husband too. "Probably."

"Is there anything else you need to know?" Lara asked.

"I think we have enough to keep us busy for a while. Before you go, though, Bella said something about the sheriff closing your case? Or was he just not working on it?"

She blew out a breath—or her version of it. "I spied on him after I contacted Bella to see what was going on. He never mentioned my case to anyone."

So, she didn't know for sure that the sheriff had officially closed the case. "And you are positive you were pushed off the road?"

She shot straight to the ceiling. "Absolutely. I saw those headlights in my rear view mirror, and they almost blinded me. When that car hit my bumper, I panicked and pressed on the brakes. Nothing I did stopped me from going down into the ravine."

"We're sorry," Gavin said. "Where was this?"

"It's off rural route 28. I can show you if you like," Lara said.

Since Bella could move with the boat, I suppose they both could ride in a car. "That would be great." I looked over at Gavin, who nodded and then stood. "Let's go."

After we bundled up, we headed to the rental car. Gavin and I piled in the front while Lara and Bella just appeared in the back.

Gavin started the engine. "Where to?"

"Go straight, and I'll tell you where to turn." We'd driven about fifteen minutes when Lara pointed to a right hand turn that Gavin took. "Go slow, as I'm not really sure where it happened. It was dark."

I probably should ask her husband to show us the site since he'd know the exact spot. Since no one was on the road, Gavin was able to take his time.

"It was on the right side of the road, correct?" I asked.

"Yes. That much I recall."

Gavin pointed to an area in which the tree branches were broken for about thirty feet off to the side of the road. "Is that it?"

"Maybe," Lara said.

"Let's stop and see," I said.

Before he was able to pull off to the side, both of our ghosts shot down the hillside. Too bad neither could hold a camera and take a picture.

Once he cut the engine, we both got out, but it was too dangerous to climb down the steep embankment.

"This has to be the spot," Gavin said. "But I don't see any skid marks."

I checked out the roadway. "Maybe she didn't apply the brakes until she was on the grassy part."

"Since the accident happened a while ago, we might not see any evidence of the tire marks. We might have better luck if I can take a look at the car," he said.

Gavin was fascinated by all kinds of vehicles. "What would that prove?" I asked.

"It's possible some paint from the other car rubbed off on Lara's car or bumper. It would let us know what color the car was that hit her."

Assuming she was hit. "That's something we should ask the sheriff if he'll even agree to talk about the case."

"True."

Lara shot up the hill. "I wish I'd never seen that. It makes my death so much more real."

I wasn't sure how that was possible, but I wasn't dead, so maybe it did. "Let's head back to town then."

Bella spent another minute looking over the site before returning, and then we drove back in relative silence. After we collected the information about where we could find her husband, her boyfriend, her brother, and a few of her good friends, we had our afternoon planned out. Between all of them, I had hoped we'd have a clue what might have happened.

"Is the sheriff's office our next stop?" Gavin asked.

"I'm thinking we should gather more information first. I want him to know that we're serious about helping, and that we aren't just two curious young people."

He smiled. "You'd make a good sleuth."

"Thank you."

Since we didn't need to drop the ghosts off, we headed to where James worked. If he was certain Lara had merely driven off the road, maybe we didn't need to bother law enforcement.

Once we parked in front of James' office, I turned to the ladies in the back. "Do you want to come in with us?" I was speaking to Lara, but no way would Bella want to be left out.

"Why?" Lara asked.

"You can tell me if he's lying about something."

She smiled. "Then sure."

Thankfully, James Finley was free to see us, but I bet he thought we were clients looking to invest. He was in his late forties and rather good looking, but his eyes appeared tired. If I had to guess, I'd say he was under a lot of stress.

"Have a seat," he said.

I introduced Gavin and myself, explaining that we weren't

there to invest, but rather we had met his brother-in-law, Cameron, on the Valentine's Day cruise to Mexico.

"Yes, my wife, who has passed, and I were supposed to be on that trip."

"I'm very sorry for your loss. I wanted to help Cameron find some closure with his sister's murder."

James stared at me, not that I blamed him. After all, I am only nineteen, and what teenager thinks she can solve a crime? I didn't feel the need to discuss my track record with him.

"The sheriff said she ran her car off the road. There was no murder involved."

Lara and Cameron claimed she was run off the road, while Stella and now James said she lost control of her car, though Stella was probably just repeating what James said. Hmm.

"James is lying—or else the sheriff is," Lara said.

I worked hard not to react. James clearly didn't hear her.

"Oh, I thought someone ran into the back of her car and pushed her down a ravine. I'm pretty sure that Lara's brother said she was in a hit-and-run accident. That implies someone was responsible for the accident."

Too bad I couldn't tell him that his wife's ghost was in the room right now, and that she'd insisted that someone murdered her.

"Cameron wants to believe that. He is having a hard time coming to grips with Lara's death."

And he wasn't? "Was Lara suicidal?"

"Heavens no."

That rules out that possibility. "Did Lara have a medical condition that would cause her to go off the road? Or did she drink?"

"Medically, she was sound, but she did drink. She often would go out after work and stay late. She called me that night and said she was going out with her girlfriend."

"Yes, I might have gone out with a friend the night of my

death, but James was the one who wasn't home most nights. I always suspected he and some coworker were doing *something* after work." Lara was clearly bitter.

This case just became juicier. Maybe James was unfaithful, and his girlfriend wanted Lara out of the way.

"Was there an autopsy done?" Gavin asked.

James' eyebrows rose. "Yes."

"Was there alcohol in her system? I ask because my mother is a medical examiner. I've grown up with these kind of things. I'm studying to be a doctor."

"I see. Yes, Lara had some alcohol in her system."

"Some maybe, but on a work night, I never had more than one glass of wine," Lara said. "Sheesh. He's acting as if I was drunk."

"What happened to the car?" Gavin asked.

"It was totaled," James said.

From the way he was tapping his fingers on his desk, he didn't want to be answering these questions. Too bad. I tried to see into his mind, but something was blocking me. That something seemed to be a combination of pain, anger, and perhaps a bit of fear. I looked over at Gavin and nodded.

When he didn't ask any more questions, I stood. "Again, I'm sorry for your loss."

It would do no good to ask who he thought murdered his wife, since he seemed to believe she'd carelessly run off the road. If that had happened to my loved one, I would have asked a few more questions of officials.

We left, but neither of us said anything until we were back in the car. I figured Lara would have an opinion about our interaction. "Your thoughts?" I asked her.

"James could have been the one to run me off the road. He didn't want to go on the cruise, you know."

No, I didn't know. "Were you fighting?"

"Yes. Like I said, he often worked late, and so I often

would go out with friends. We had a great life for the first ten years. Then things kind of went downhill once our careers started to pick up."

"No children, I take it?" I asked.

She shook her head.

Gavin started the engine and looked over at me. "Where to next, ladies?"

"We need more information about the night Lara died, which means we need to hear more people's take on the situation. We're getting a lot of conflicting information."

"You mean false information," Lara said.

"Possibly." We couldn't conclude what really happened, especially since Lara couldn't remember anything leading up to the incident. It was possible another car came up behind her with his brights on. She might have been temporarily blinded and lost control.

"How about if we speak with your brother? He would have spoken to the sheriff. I'm interested in why your brother thinks you were killed whereas James does not."

"Sure." Lara pointed us in the direction of his office.

I wasn't optimistic that Dr. Hackett could see us in the middle of his work day, but he might if he remembered that I helped solve Bella's murder.

chapter five

THERE WAS ONLY one person in the office when Gavin and I arrived at Dr. Hackett's office.

"I'll see if my brother is busy."

Before I could nod or shake my head, Lara was gone, with Bella right behind her. It had to be hard seeing your loved ones in pain and not being able to communicate with them. I knew I would have a hard time with it. Thankfully, at least Iggy, if not a few other people in town would be able to see me when I came back as a ghost, and Bella at least had been able to use some voodoo power to kind of communicate with her dad.

Gavin and I went up to the receptionist, who probably thought we weren't much more than ten years old considering her age.

"May I help you?" she asked.

Here came the hard part. "I'm a friend of Dr. Hackett's. Well, friend might be a stretch. We were on a cruise to Mexico together. I just need five minutes of his time. It's about his sister, Lara." I said all of that in one breath.

"Oh, I see. He's with a patient, but if you take a seat, I'll ask him if he can squeeze you in."

"Thank you." It was the best we could hope for.

Once we found seats away from the other person, Gavin leaned over. "What are you going to ask him?"

"What he knows about Lara's death, and why he believes she was murdered. I'm hoping he saw the crashed vehicle so that he can tell us the condition of the rear of the car."

He smiled. "Ever the optimist, I see."

I lightly punched him in the arm. "It's called wishful thinking."

Not wanting to attract too much attention, I decided to play on my phone while we waited. Less than ten minutes later, Dr. Hackett's office door opened, and an elderly woman exited.

The receptionist motioned we go in. I inhaled, hoping for a good outcome. When we entered, our two ghosts were circling the poor man. Why, I didn't know. They should have waited with us, though if they had, one of them would have wanted to chat, which would have made us look odd if we'd answered.

It was possible waiting rooms bothered them for some reason, but did they really want to watch someone work on feet?

When Cameron Hackett looked up from his desk, he did a double take. "You? Aren't you the photographer from the cruise?"

His thoughts were quite open. Surprise, distrust, and residual sadness laced his mind. "Yes. Your receptionist said you could spare five minutes. It's about Lara."

"You have news about who caused the hit-and-run?" Hope surged through him as he waved us to sit down.

On the off chance he might kick us out if I made up a story, I decided to tell him the truth. I trusted him a lot more than James. "Some news. I know you'll think I'm crazy, but I can see ghosts. In fact, Lara is in the room with us right now." *Please believe me.*

He shook his head. "Ghosts don't exist."

It came as no surprise that a wave of doubt entered his mind. "Ask me a question that only you and she would know the answer to."

Cameron Hackett wiped his brow. "Where is she?"

I pointed to the corner, but then Lara moved closer. "Actually, now she's in front of you."

"Lara?" His voice cracked.

"Oh, Cameron. I am so sorry you suffered because of me."

I repeated what Lara said, but that only made his lower lip tremble. "Go ahead. Ask her something."

"Um. What was the name of our first dog?"

She smiled. "Rover."

When I said the name, I thought he'd come apart at the seams. "She's really here?"

"Yes. Lara wanted to see you, of course, but she also needs to find out who killed her," I said.

"I don't know. I wish I did."

"Why is it that you believe your sister was a victim of a hit-and-run when the sheriff does not?"

"I think he's covering up something." His hands fisted as his breathing increased. "I just don't know what."

Accusing law enforcement of something illegal wasn't what I expected to hear. Cameron looked around, as if searching the room enough would let him see his sister.

"Would it be better if we came back later? I know you have a patient out there." And he looked like he needed some time to come to grip with things.

His hands even shook. "Yes, I'd appreciate that. I need to wrap my head around the fact that Lara is alive—I mean is here. Even though she can communicate, she's still dead, right?"

"I consider ghosts as being in some intermediary state rather than being alive or dead." Okay, the person was technically dead, but she wasn't lacking the ability to think or speak to those who could hear her. So would Cameron think of her as being dead? Of course, but to me, Bella, Lara, and Lorenzo were kind of alive.

I couldn't blame Cameron for being so distraught. The whole idea of the existence of ghosts was mind blowing. I'd grown up with the idea of the occult, so seeing ghosts didn't shock me too much.

"How does she look?" he asked.

I wasn't about to say she looked terrible because of the accident. Describing the condition of any ghost to someone was next to impossible, and understanding it was even more difficult. "Rather see-through."

"Oh. That makes sense, I guess." He ran his fingers through his hair. "I'm sorry I'm such a mess right now. Perhaps you could come to the house tonight around six? Lara knows where I live."

I figure this might be his way of testing us. "We can do that. She gave us your address."

Gavin and I stood. At least Cameron didn't deny that his sister had been murdered. That was two votes in favor of someone running her off the road and two against if I didn't count Stella. Hopefully, tonight we'd learn a few more answers.

On the way out, we thanked the receptionist. Bella floated in front of me as we stepped into the hallway. "You could have asked him a few more questions. I think he knows more."

I waited until we were outside before I answered. "He might, but he needed time to compose himself. We have plenty of other people to see. By the time we stop at his house tonight, he will hopefully be in a better frame of mind to answer our questions."

Gavin wrapped an arm around my waist. "You're sure Cameron Hackett is innocent of harming his sister?"

"Yes. He has an open mind. I'd know if he had any part in Lara's death."

"That's good to hear."

Lara harrumphed. "I could have told you that. Cameron and I were always close."

"I sensed that," I said. "Who should we talk with next?"

"Girlfriends always know a lot," Bella said.

"Sounds good. Lara, who might be home?"

"Let's try Karen Dimple," Lara suggested.

Since I knew no one, I had to trust her. We climbed into the car, and I shivered at the cold snaking up my legs. I wasn't built for this weather. "Where does Karen live?"

Lara gave Gavin directions. It took less than fifteen minutes to reach Karen's place. She lived in a sprawling home on the edge of town that faced the mountains. I could only imagine that the different plays of light would be amazing to photograph. "How open is Karen to the idea of ghosts?"

"Not at all."

That stunk, but I bet Lara would have said the same thing about her brother. We pulled into her friend's driveway, and we had to walk a bit to reach the front door. Gavin knocked.

A man in a suit answered. "Yes?"

"We'd like to speak with Karen. It's about her friend, Lara." I felt it best to be upfront.

His brow rose. "You knew Lara?"

Just because I was nineteen shouldn't eliminate me from having known her, but I didn't comment on it. "I know her brother."

His lips pressed together. Clearly, he wasn't pleased with the intrusion. He motioned we enter the foyer but not to go any farther.

Once he disappeared from view, I looked up at Gavin. "I don't think I've ever been to a home with a butler. That must be nice."

"I have, but remember, I grew up in Miami."

"True." I turned to Lara. "You didn't tell me she was so rich."

"It has no bearing on my case. Besides, it's her husband's money. Karen is different. You'll like her."

A woman in a jogging outfit with her hair pulled back into a messy bun came down the stairs. "Hi, I'm Karen. You're here about Lara?"

"Yes. We have some questions about her death."

Karen looked off to the side, but I didn't have the sense she was guilty of harming her friend. However, she was hiding something. I could only hope that Karen held the key to what was going on.

"Come in, but I don't know what I can tell you. The sheriff said she just ran off the road and hit a tree."

Really? He was sticking with that story—though it could be true.

She led us through a magnificent living room. Large paintings filled the walls, and tall sculptures sat in the corners. The floor to ceiling windows displayed a magnificent view of the mountains. A definite wow.

"It's cozier in here," Karen said as we moved into a small den. "My husband, Michael, loves fancy things, but I prefer it simple."

She picked up a remote and lit the gas fireplace. Thank you! I sat in the chair closest to the heat while Gavin took the sofa. The two ladies floated above us.

"You might as well tell her I'm here," Lara said.

I nodded. I went through the same spiel I did for Cameron Hackett. The whole time I watched Karen's face. Instead of grief, I spotted disgust, possibly because she thought I was making a mockery of her friend's death. But that couldn't be helped.

"You talk to ghosts?" Karen huffed out her question.

I expected her to say that. "On occasion."

Lara moved between us. "Tell her thank you for the ruby ring she gave me for Christmas."

"Okay." I faced her friend. "Lara said thank you for the ruby ring you gave her at Christmas."

Karen's demeanor completely changed to one of total confusion. "How could you know that?"

I had said I could talk to ghosts. "Lara just told me."

"That can't be. She's dead."

"I know. It doesn't matter what you believe. What matters is that Lara asked another ghost if I could help solve her murder." I held up a hand. "You told me that Lara drove off the road all by herself, but that is not what she told me."

Karen's mouth opened and then closed. "I figured it was true, because Lara had been acting rather strangely right before the accident. She was rather distraught, which was why I assumed Lara lost control of her car."

That matched what the waitress told us. "Distraught over what?"

Karen sat up straighter. "She was searching through her father-in-law's attic and found something. In case she didn't mention it, he'd recently passed."

"She told us."

Karen's brows rose. "Did she tell you what she found?"

Aha. This might be something. "No, because the accident somehow caused her to lose her memory for the few days leading up to her death. What did she find?"

"I didn't see it, but she said it was some kind of photo album."

My mind raced, thinking all sorts of nefarious scenarios.

"What was in the album?" Gavin asked.

Karen looked off to the side again. "I find it hard to believe, but she said it showed pictures of people who had wounds in their necks."

Considering I spent a week with a vampire ghost, I couldn't help but go there. "Did she say how they received these wounds?"

Karen rolled her eyes. "She was convinced that a vampire bit them."

Lara sucked in a breath. "I think I remember that."

As much as I wanted to have that conversation, now wasn't the best time. "I recently found out that vampires are real. And trust me, no one was more surprised that I was."

Karen chuckled, but it held no joy. "Seriously?"

"You have no idea what's out in the world. I think it's kept quiet to keep people from panicking."

Karen's chin dipped. "What's next? Are you going to say that aliens have already landed and are walking among us?"

Oh, boy. "No, but only because I've never seen one." I leaned forward. "Did Lara have any idea why her father-in-law had this album?"

"Why don't you ask her? She's here, right?"

I was wondering when she'd throw that back at me, but I'd just told her that Lara had lost her memory. "The last thing she remembers is packing for her cruise. Everything near to the time of her death is blank." Other than the headlights coming up behind her. Any discussion with the father-in-law would have occurred quite a while ago—when Lara still had her memory. However, she didn't remember the album. Interesting.

"I don't know anything more than that. I wish I did. I'd ask James, her husband."

"We've spoken to him, but he didn't mention any album."

Gavin leaned forward and then glanced between us. "Could the album have contained evidence of a crime? Like by a town councilmember or some important person breaking the law?"

I didn't see the connection between possible vampire bites

and a white collar crime. Not unless the councilmember was a vampire.

Karen shrugged. "I never saw the album, and Lara didn't say much more about it. That could be because I didn't take her seriously, and I'm sorry about that now."

"May I ask what Lara's father-in-law did for a living?" If he was a medical examiner, he might have wanted to hide photos of the vampire bites.

"He owned a tree farm."

That blew my theory. "James said Lara was out the night of her accident. Do you know who she was with?"

"Yes. Me. Lara asked that we go out so we could discuss her husband. She was confused about her feelings for someone other than James."

That could have been the reason why she was distraught too. "We've heard it was Daniel Weintraub, the lawyer."

Karen stilled. "Yes. How did you know?"

I thought it was obvious. I nodded to where Lara was floating about. "She told me."

"Did Lara have a lot to drink that night?" Gavin asked.

"I told you guys. I never have more than one drink on a work night. Sheesh."

I ignored her outburst.

"Not really. We always limited our drinks on a work night." Karen planted her hands on her thighs. "I wish I knew more. I really do, but I don't."

I believed her, especially since it matched Lara's claim. "Thank you for your time."

"That's it?" Lara asked.

Bella swooped in. "Lara, we can always come back if we have to. We don't want to overstay our visit."

That almost cracked me up. When Bella was alive, she never cared about doing something the proper way. I stood.

"If you think of anything that might relate to Lara's death, we're at the Mountain View Hotel."

"Sure."

I hope that if I died, my friends would be more anxious to learn what really happened to me. Karen escorted us out, and once more the cold air shocked my system. While Netwood was pretty, it wasn't where I wanted to settle down.

If Gavin and I tied the knot, once he received his internship, I could only hope it would be to someplace warm.

I rushed to the car and slid in. Gavin jumped in and cranked up the engine. I immediately turned up the heat, not that is was working yet.

Bella appeared in the back. "Why didn't you tell her that you personally knew a vampire?"

"I don't think she would have believed me. It was enough that I told her I could communicate with Lara."

"Karen is super nice but kind of set in her ways," Lara said. "In fact, I used to be that way too."

"Most people are set in their way until someone or something shakes them out of it."

Gavin pulled out of the driveway. "Where to next, ladies?"

chapter six

"I THINK we need to find out why Sheriff Schlemmer is so convinced that I wasn't run off the road," Lara said.

"I would love to know what proof the sheriff has that you did it all by yourself, since your brother believes another vehicle was involved." I realize our chances of him telling us much were slim, but we had to try.

"I'll be right there with you when you find out," she said.

"I don't know why I'm asking, but I'm guessing the good sheriff isn't the type to believe in the occult?"

She laughed. "That would be a hard no."

My stomach grumbled, and I was immediately reminded of my cousin, Glinda, who was always hungry. "How about we attempt to see the sheriff and then grab something to eat?"

Naturally, I was speaking to Gavin since ghosts didn't eat.

"Works for me," he said.

Gavin found a parking spot about two blocks from the sheriff's office. When we entered, I was a bit disappointed that it didn't have that cozy feel that our Witch's Cove sheriff's office did. There was no elderly woman knitting at the reception desk with a plate of delicious smelling cookies next to her.

Instead, we had to deal with someone at a desk sitting behind a piece of plexiglass.

"May I help you?" The young officer didn't even bother looking up. He was typing something into the computer instead of making sure we weren't a threat or something. Really?

"I'd like to speak with the sheriff about a murder."

That caught the man's attention, and he finally took notice of us. "Oh. Who was murdered?"

"I'll tell the sheriff."

He sent out massive signals of irritation. "Your names?"

"Rihanna Samuels and Gavin Sanchez."

"One moment." He typed something else into his computer and then returned his attention to us. "Please have a seat over there, and I'll let you know if the sheriff is free."

And here I thought it was cold outside. The two of us sat. No surprise Lara and Bella took off to the back, hopefully to check out the Netwood sheriff. I was looking forward to learning what he was up to. "What are our chances of speaking with him?" I asked Gavin, though I don't know how he'd know.

He grabbed my hand. "Don't worry. We don't need his information."

"We do. The sheriff is the one who claims no one ran Lara off the road. Why is that?" I looked around at the empty sitting room. It seemed as if Netwood was just another sleepy town, so how busy could he be?

The gentleman—and I'm being generous here—from behind the glass enclosed desk came out. "The sheriff is busy, but the deputy will see you."

Really? The sheriff couldn't take five minutes to learn about a murder? The deputy was better than no one, I guess. "Thanks."

I looked around for our two ghosts, but the sheriff must really be doing something important—like conferring with the mayor or some bigwig, or they would have been back by now. Hopefully, they could find us. So far, Bella seemed to have a sixth sense regarding my location.

The officer led us to an office with a sign that read, Deputy Dusty Denison. His name had a nice ring to it. The officer knocked and then opened the door.

"Two to see you about a murder."

"Thank you, Jim."

The deputy motioned we take a seat. I wish I had a way of contacting Lara and Bella, but if they weren't here, I was sure they were someplace important.

"You want to report a murder?"

I looked over at Gavin who nodded his encouragement. "Actually, I wanted to find out about Lara Finley's murder. Some say she drove off the road that night, hit a tree, and died, while others are convinced someone ran into the back of her car and forced her off the road. I would like the official take."

The deputy dipped his chin. "I'm afraid I'm not at liberty to discuss that case."

"Why? It's not an ongoing investigation since I heard the sheriff is claiming she drove off the road."

The deputy, who was about fifty, leaned forward. "Who are you again? And I don't mean your names."

As I opened my mouth, guess who flew in? Yup, Lara and Bella. Good. I looked up at Lara. "We are friends of Lara's brother, Cameron Hackett. We want to help find out what really happened that night. If no one caused her to go down that ravine, has anyone figured out why she drove off the road?"

He huffed out a laugh. "Two teenagers are going to help figure that out?"

This wasn't the first time I've seen this kind of skepticism. I didn't mind if he underestimated me. It came in handy sometimes.

Lara floated in front of me. "Remind him that his teenage son helped uncover some thefts at a department store last year."

"We're going to try. Though wasn't it your *teenage* son who helped solve some theft case at a department store?"

His eyes nearly bugged out. "How did you know about that?"

"Tell him," Lara urged.

"Lara told me."

"Why would she have told you that?"

Here goes. "Because Lara is a ghost. In fact, she's in the room right now. She just told me about your son. And before you say ghosts don't exist, I'm sure she can tell me other things about you." I leaned forward. "Look, all we want to know is whether Lara imagined a car ramming her car bumper or not."

The deputy turned a few shades of red. "I didn't investigate the case. The sheriff did, but he told me that she just lost control."

"On a straight away?" Gavin said.

The deputy squirmed in his chair. "She had alcohol in her system."

"That again? It was one drink from an hour before I stepped in the car," she said. "Oh, wait. I just regained a bit of my memory!"

I wanted to cheer, but that would have raised too many questions.

"Was it over the legal limit?" Gavin asked.

"I don't know." The deputy looked a bit sheepish.

"Could she have been texting, become distracted, and lost control?" I asked.

"No, Rihanna. My phone died at the restaurant. You can

ask Karen." She smiled, probably because her memory was slowly returning.

I wish she'd remembered sooner.

"I bet she was," the deputy said. Once more, I didn't need to be a mind reader to tell he was making that up.

"Where is her phone now? In evidence? Oh, wait. No. There hasn't been a crime. Did you return the phone in her car to her husband?"

Gavin nudged me with his foot. Clearly, I'd shot into attack mode, which wouldn't help us receive any kind of cooperation.

"I'd have to check with the sheriff." Deputy Denison said that with more confidence. Clearly, he was losing patience with us.

"Where is her car now?" Gavin asked, sounding like a well-caring person.

"It's probably been crushed. After all, she died over a month ago."

Seriously? A small-town junk yard had the machinery to crush a car? Not to mention it could be evidence in a crime. "What kind of car did she drive?" I asked.

"I don't know."

"It was a one-year old BMW," Lara said.

"Lara just told me it was a fairly new BMW. I would think they'd strip it down and sell the parts instead of crushing it."

The deputy mumbled something. "You'd have to speak with the sheriff."

"We tried."

Gavin placed a hand on mine. "Do you know where they took the car to be *crushed*?"

"Probably to Jake's Auto on Third and Sampson Avenue."

"What were the road conditions like the night of her death? Was it snowing?" he asked.

"I didn't read the report, but it might have been."

"Thank you. You've been a big help." Sometimes, I couldn't help keep my sarcasm in check.

"That's all?" Lara asked.

Since the deputy probably already thought I was crazy, I saw no reason not to answer her. "What would you have me ask him?"

"Did my husband try to find out the truth?"

I wasn't sure she really wanted to hear the answer but I asked the deputy anyway.

"Sure. James came in a few times, but the sheriff told him there was nothing to investigate."

"Thanks."

Not satisfied in the least, we left. I was interested to hear what Bella thought about all of this, and also what the ladies had to say about the sheriff. "How about we sit in the car for a bit before we find a place to eat? That way we can chat."

"Sure," Lara answered.

The ghosts instantly moved to the car. I looked over at Gavin. "What are your thoughts?"

"Something isn't right, though I'm not sure the deputy knows the truth."

"I kind of agree. Let's hope Bella and Lara can tell us more." When we reached the car, I was happy to be out of the chilly wind.

I turned around to face our ghosts. "Tell me about the sheriff."

"He was by himself," Lara said. "I think he didn't want to see you."

That was an interesting twist.

"Tell her the best part," Bella said.

"Oh, yeah. He called someone and said some visitors were in town asking about my accident."

I looked over at Gavin. "If Lara had driven off the road all by herself, why would the sheriff care?"

"That's a good question." Gavin faced Lara. "Did he sound scared, unconcerned, or happy during the call?"

She chuckled. "Definitely not happy. He sounded more worried than anything."

"Since it's way past lunchtime, how about Gavin and I eat something, and you two head over to Jake's place to see if you can find your car."

"You got it." And then they were gone.

"Darn. I should have asked her for a restaurant suggestion."

Gavin smiled. "I saw a place that looks interesting." He pushed open his car door, and I followed suit.

The restaurant was only two blocks away and was really cute. "It's too bad your mom couldn't ask the medical examiner in Netwood about Lara's autopsy."

"That would raise a few eyebrows. The only time my mother calls another medical examiner is if she isn't sure what killed the person."

That was too bad. "We know what killed Lara—the tree she ran into."

"True. Don't worry, we'll figure something out."

I had to admit, I hadn't expected Gavin to be so interested in this sleuthing stuff, though when he became a doctor, he would be doing a lot of investigating.

The restaurant was mostly empty, so we were seated quickly. The hostess handed us menus and told us our server would be right with us.

"I wish I'd thought to bring my notepad. I need to write down what we learned from each person," I said.

"That's a great idea, but who do we even have as a suspect?" he asked.

I had to think. "If I had to guess, I might say James, only because he hasn't hounded the sheriff for more information about Lara's death."

"You know, you have to be prepared that she might have become distracted and actually run off the road. If she was driving more than forty miles an hour on that dark road, even a two second distraction could have caused her wheel to turn. We need to find out if it was snowing. I'm not taking the word of the deputy who clearly was making it up as he went."

"I couldn't agree more. Road conditions would be a factor. Hopefully, Lara will remember."

"Regardless of what she says, we need to look it up."

He was right. It was best to double check all facts.

Since the waitress would be over shortly, we looked over the menu. Apparently, breakfast was served all day, so I chose a French Toast plate, while Gavin opted for a cheese omelet. I wished I could have enjoyed the town, but my mind refused to stop spinning. I was like my cousin, Glinda, in that respect.

Gavin pulled out his phone. "I want to jot down who we've at least spoken to. Then we should rank them like Glinda does in regards to how likely they are to have had something to do with Lara's death."

"Great. I don't think her friend Karen had anything to do with Lara's dying, though she did imply that Lara could have been distracted because of that album she found." Or it could have been because of Lara's confusion over her relationship with her husband.

"Ah, yes," Gavin said. "The album that contained pictures of people with puncture marks in their necks."

"We should have asked if the images were of living or dead people."

"I had the sense they were alive," he said.

"If it wasn't a vampire, what could have caused those marks?"

Gavin pointed a finger at me. "If we can have a glimpse of the album, I can take a picture of a few of them and send them to my mom. She might have an idea."

I smiled. "That's the best idea we've had today."

chapter seven

ONCE WE FINISHED OUR MEAL, we discussed the next person we needed to interview.

"I'm thinking we should see what Daniel Weintraub has to say," I said.

"I'm game, but only if we see him at his office," Gavin said.

Gavin was always such a protector. "I agree that we need to treat everyone as a suspect." I smiled. "Except the people I'm sure are innocent."

Gavin chuckled. "Do you think he is one of the innocent ones?"

"How would I know? I haven't even met him."

"Just checking. I'll give him a call."

"Good. You might have better luck than me getting in to see him."

"Why's that?"

I shrugged. "Your voice is deeper."

Yes, I was kidding, but I had the sense a lawyer's office might take a man more seriously. Thank goodness, Gavin was tall, broad shouldered, and looked a lot older than twenty, or we might be told to go home and come back when we were older.

Gavin contacted the office, but the receptionist told him that Mr. Weintraub was booked for the day.

"When can we see him?" Gavin glanced over at me and shrugged. "It's about Lara Finley's death. We're friends of her brother." He listened for a few seconds. "Yes, five fifteen would be perfect. Thank you." Gavin disconnected and smiled. "We're in."

"That was easy. Did the person you spoke with even consult with Daniel? Or did Lara's name alone get us the appointment?"

"The secretary just seemed to know he'd want to speak with us."

That was a stroke of luck. "I have no basis for saying this, but if he ran her off the road, he'd stonewall us for longer than a few hours."

"Let's hope you're right."

After we paid for our meal, we headed back to the hotel since we had some time before we could interview Daniel Weintraub. "Let's hope the ladies have information for us."

"They haven't disappointed us yet."

I smiled. "No, they have not."

When we entered our room, both Bella and Lara were waiting for us. Considering they were finished with the junk yard search, I thought they would have found us in the restaurant. Perhaps they realized that having a conversation with others around would be awkward for us.

"Any luck?" I asked.

"Yes. My car is at Jake's, but it was terrible for me to look at it. The front was completely demolished."

Bella moved in front of her and scrunched up her face. "There was blood all over the steering wheel."

"I imagine there was." I'm sure Lara didn't need to relive her death. "How about the rear bumper? Could you tell if a car hit it?"

"I couldn't tell," Bella said. "Other cars were crowded all around it, but if the bumper was smashed, it could have been due to those cars nearby."

"That stinks," I said.

"I'd still like to see it," Gavin said. "There could be clues you two didn't notice."

I nodded. "How far is Jake's Auto from here?" We certainly didn't want to miss our interview with Daniel Weintraub.

"Ten minutes maybe?" Lara said.

"How about coming with us and showing us where your car is?" Gavin asked.

"You bet."

The four of us piled into our rental—if the ghosts' floating movement could be considered piling in. Gavin then followed Lara's instructions to the auto shop. Once there, we told the man we were looking for a rear bumper for a 2021 BMW. We followed Ed out through the back of the office to the junkyard part of the business. I'm glad we were honest about what we were looking for since a possible killer still was out there. The last time I'd asked a lot of questions about a murder, someone tried to prevent me from ever revealing the truth again.

"You're in luck. Had one come in about a month ago. Front's a little bent, but the rear might be in good shape. I'll show you."

Lara flew over to her car and naturally Bella was right next to her. When Ed showed us a different BMW, Gavin thanked him. How odd that another car like Lara's was in the lot.

"I'll check it out. Mind if we look around? I love old cars."

"Sure. Let me know if you need something."

I had the sense Ed didn't think we'd be spending any money, so he saw no reason to spend time with us, and that worked for me.

"I'll pretend to check out the rear and then make my way to Lara's car," Gavin said.

"Good plan. I'll just wander around."

Bella and Lara came over. "That's not my car," Lara told me.

"I know, but we couldn't tell Ed that. I'll go over to your car and then call Gavin over."

Happy with my plan, I followed the ghosts to where Lara's car was located. In case Ed was watching, I pretended to look at a few cars. When I arrived at hers, I realized the dilemma. Her car was wedged between two others, but the front was definitely destroyed. I'd let Gavin crawl between the cars in order to inspect the rear bumper.

"Hey, Gavin, check this one out." I waved to him and he trotted over.

Gavin looked at the cars. "That's not good. Let me see if I can move closer."

"Take a picture of the bumper if you can."

"I'll try."

Gavin climbed over one car and checked out the back of Lara's car. "How does it look?" I called.

"Hard to say. It's dented for sure, but that could have been a result of other cars in the lot smashing against it when the cars were placed here."

"Take a picture anyway. There might be paint scrapings that don't match the cars around it." I didn't think that would hold up in court, but it might prove that Lara had been run off the road.

Gavin did as I asked. When he finished, he climbed back out.

Just then Ed came out and marched toward us. "We have company," I mumbled to Gavin.

"No problem. I'll tell him I didn't find what I was looking for. I wanted a more pristine bumper."

We met Ed half way to his office. When Gavin told him about the bumper not being the right kind, Ed clearly didn't believe him. All I could read in his mind was something about a phone call and the word *stop.* What that meant, I didn't know, but it didn't sound good.

We thanked Ed and left. As soon as we slipped into our rental, Gavin took off.

"What did that guy want?" Bella asked.

I told the three of them what I thought I heard him thinking.

"When I saw my car, images of me being pushed more than once entered my mind's eye. I kind of remember speeding up to get away from the person, but then they just rammed my car harder."

"Lara, I didn't see that kind of damage," Gavin said.

"I'm not lying."

I wanted to hold her hand. "We know, Lara, but the mind can play tricks on us. We'll get to the bottom of this. I promise." Or I hoped we would.

I turned to Gavin. "Why do you think Ed was thinking the word *stop*?"

"I don't know," he said. "Do you want me to say that someone called him and told him to stop us from investigating?"

"Yes. That's what I was thinking, but who would have called? Or did Ed call this person to say someone was snooping around Lara's car? If so, the person he called could have been the killer."

He glanced over at me. "Let's say it was. That doesn't narrow down our suspect list. The caller could have been the sheriff, the deputy, James, or maybe Daniel Weintraub. They all know we are here to investigate Lara's accident. If she was murdered—which we believe—the killer would be sweating bullets right now."

"You're right. I haven't worked on that many cases, but when people take one look at me, they always think I'm too young to do much harm. No one knows I can sometimes read minds or that we have two ghosts—one of whom is the accident victim—with us."

Gavin smiled. "That's true. We're like superheroes in disguise."

That was taking it a bit too far. "Perhaps."

"That's not true, Rihanna," Bella said. "My killer took you very seriously."

"You have a point."

When we returned to town, it was almost time to visit Daniel Weintraub. I turned to Lara. "Where is Daniel's office?"

She gave us directions. "You can't miss it. It's the tallest building in Netwood."

"Is there anything we should be aware of?" I asked.

"Like what?"

"Is Daniel easy going or quick to anger? Is he a private person or more open? Stuff like that."

"He's cautious, ambitious, and highly competitive."

A man like that might decide if he couldn't have Lara, no one could. "I'll keep that in mind."

We parked back at the hotel and walked to Daniel Weintraub's office. Naturally, our friendly ghosts joined us. I didn't bother asking Lara if Daniel believed in ghosts, as I was sure she'd say no.

No surprise, once inside the office, we were asked to take a seat. Even though it should have been a little after office hours, another gentleman was in the seating area.

"I'll see what Daniel is up to," Lara said the moment we sat down.

"Do you need me to keep you company?" Bella asked me.

That was sweet, but it wasn't as if I could carry on a

conversation with her while the man was within earshot. Sometimes I wondered if maybe she'd forgotten that she was dead. I slightly shook my head no, and then Bella left.

Gavin leaned over. "Do you want to take a bet on whether he thinks Lara was killed or not?"

I inhaled. "I'm thinking he won't be sure, but if you are close to a person, you'd have a sense whether they were the type to become distracted, were suicidal, or a possible victim of an assault."

"I agree. I'm guessing you'll do the usual ask-a-question-that-only-Lara-knows-the-answer-to thing so you can prove ghosts exist?"

"Why not? If even a part of the person believes Lara could be in the room, they might be more willing to tell the truth."

Gavin clasped my hand and squeezed. "That's my girl."

Less than ten minutes later, a tall man came out of the back, followed by our two ghosts. Lara pointing to Daniel and smiled. "What do you think?"

I wasn't about to say he was good looking in front of Gavin. Even if I did, I'd lose some credibility with Daniel, because he'd think I was talking to myself.

He came over to us with his hand extended. "I'm Daniel Weintraub."

We both shook his hand and introduced ourselves.

"Come into my office."

I figured he wouldn't want to talk about such a sensitive topic in the lobby. The secretary, wearing a winter coat and scarf, entered the seating area. The man who'd been in there stood and gave her a kiss on the cheek. So, he wasn't a client. Good.

Once we were seated in front of his desk, Daniel Weintraub faced us. "You said this is about Lara?"

"Yes. The short of it is that I met her brother, Cameron, on a cruise to Mexico. When I noticed how sad he was, I asked him about it. He said his sister had been killed in a hit-and-run accident right before the cruise, and that his brother-in-law suggested Cameron take their place."

Mr. Weintraub had a bottle of water on his desk, and he chugged down a large portion of it. "I heard that, but I haven't spoken with Cameron. I'm still not over Lara's death."

"Do you believe someone hit her from behind and ran her off the road?" Gavin asked.

"I want to believe it. The sheriff is insistent that Lara must have been texting or had too much to drink. The roads had a fresh dusting of snow on them, so her tires could have skidded. If so, she would have gone down the embankment. Being steep, she wouldn't have been able to stop until she hit the tree."

There were some issues with his statement. "Did they find her phone in the car or in her purse?"

Mr. Weintraub looked stunned. "I don't know. It's not like me not to ask." He pulled out a tablet and made a note.

"Did the sheriff tell you the level of alcohol in her blood?" Gavin asked.

"Sheriff Schlemmer was rather tight-lipped about the facts in the case. Remember, I'm not a relative."

"Did you have the chance to look at the bumper on Lara's car?" Gavin asked. "We checked it out, and it's possible she was rammed from behind."

I'm not sure we could conclude she was rammed from behind without testing the scrapings on her bumper with the other cars close to her in the junkyard, but it was okay to call his bluff.

"Where are you two from?" he asked.

It was inevitable that he'd wonder why we were so interested, and how we knew so much. I looked over at Gavin and a small smile lifted his lips. He knew what was coming.

"We're from Florida, but a friend of mine was visited by

Lara's ghost, and she told us all about you, James, and the accident."

chapter **eight**

"LARA'S GHOST told you about the accident?" Mr. Weintraub huffed out a laugh. "Okay, kids, I'm afraid you'll have to leave." For a lawyer, Mr. Weintraub wasn't very good at controlling his facial expressions, because his brows pinched, and his lips pressed together.

Lara floated in between us. "He's not normally this rude. Tell him that our first kiss was at the bottom of Canyon Road. Maybe he'll believe that I'm here."

"Lara is in this room right now. She asked me to remind you that your first kiss was at the bottom of Canyon Road."

I hoped he'd say that ghosts were real now, but most people needed more proof. When his face paled, Lara passed through him, and he shivered. Even I thought it was weird to see her do that.

"In case you're wondering what that cold sensation was," I said, "that was Lara joining her body with yours for a few seconds. Ghosts do that." That sounded better than saying she passed through his body.

Like everyone we'd met had done, he looked around. "She's here?"

Finally, I think he was starting to believe what I was claiming was true. "Yes."

He stabbed his fingers through his neatly combed hair. "Wow. I always assumed that when someone died, that was it."

"A lot of people think that. Why wouldn't they? No one has proof to the contrary."

"I guess that makes sense," Mr. Weintraub said.

"This is a lot to take in, so let me give you a little background. Lara *visited* my cruise ship roommate and asked for her help in solving her murder."

He seemed to ponder that comment. "How did Lara know this roommate would be able to see her, because I can't see her."

I guess I forgot that part. "Yeah. About that. My roommate was murdered on the cruise and is now a ghost. And ghosts can communicate with fellow ghosts."

"So now we're talking about two ghosts?"

I was losing him. "Yes, Bella is here too."

"Hmm. What did Lara tell your roommate?"

I went through most of what we knew. "Here's the problem. Lara doesn't remember a lot of what happened the few days leading up to the night of her death, but her friend, Karen, filled us in."

"Did what she tell you help? Because if so, let me know."

"Her information wasn't all that helpful."

Gavin shifted in his seat. "Before we get into the one item that was useful, can you tell us what evidence the sheriff has that led him to believe Lara drove off the road by herself? For example, did he say her bumper was in perfect condition, which meant there wasn't another vehicle? Or was it the fact he didn't find any tire marks?" Gavin asked.

"I didn't ask too many questions. Even if I had, Sheriff Schlemmer would have only told her family. Did you speak with the sheriff yet?"

"We tried. We ended up speaking with Deputy Denison. He told us that there was no evidence of foul play. Rihanna and I had the sense he was repeating what the sheriff told him to say."

Mr. Weintraub slammed a hand on the desk. "I knew there was a coverup, but I couldn't prove it. Where is Lara now?"

"Right next to your desk," I told him.

He looked to his left.

"No, on the other side."

"Oh. Lara, if what you think really happened, could the photo album you found have anything to do with it?" he asked her.

On instinct, I grabbed Gavin's hand, awaiting her answer.

She looked over at us. "Tell him I don't remember the album, but Karen said I'd found it in my father-in-law's attic. Ask Daniel what was so special about the album. Maybe he knows."

I relayed her comment. "Did you ever see the album?"

"Briefly, but it was odd."

"What was odd about it?" Gavin asked.

"Inside were photos of people with small wounds on their necks."

Once more, my thoughts jumped to vampires. If Lorenzo Bambini III, a vampire ghost, were here, he might be able to clarify a few things for us. Lorenzo had explained that much of the lore I'd seen on television wasn't accurate. No surprise there.

"Did Lara know why her father-in-law had these photos?" I asked.

"No, but she was determined to find out."

Ah. That was what might have gotten her killed. Or else I was grasping at straws.

"Did she ask you to help figure out what the album meant?" I asked.

Daniel Weintraub searched the room. It was almost as if he believed if he looked hard enough, he'd see some part of her—however faint. "Yes, but I told her I needed more facts. I am a lawyer, after all."

"That makes sense."

"Did she ask James about this album?" Gavin questioned. "After all, his father had it."

"She did, but James claimed he knew nothing about it."

I turned to Gavin. "I wonder if she told her brother."

"I might have," Lara piped up. "Why can't I remember things?"

I told Mr. Weintraub what Lara said, and sympathy oozed out of him.

"Lara, you had a traumatic brain injury," Gavin explained. "It's not uncommon for a person who's been hit on the head to be unable to recall the details of the incident."

"Will my memory return?" she asked.

I let Gavin answer. He was the medical student. "Since some of it has already started to surface, it's possible but not guaranteed."

Bella moved in front of me. "Ask the boyfriend guy here about the status of his relationship with Lara before she was in the accident."

I nodded. Answering her directly might cause more confusion for him, even though I'd just told him both Bella and Lara were in the room. "Lara told me that you were the one to suggest she go on a cruise with her husband to figure out what she wanted, which was to choose between the two of you."

He huffed out a laugh, but it contained little joy. "Thanks, Lara for airing our issues."

I needed to defend her. "Lara only told us that so we could figure out who killed her."

Mr. Weintraub dipped his chin. "Does she think I ran her off the road?"

"She doesn't know who did, but I don't think she believes it was you. I kept pressing her for information about everyone she was involved with, and she just told us about you two. For all we know, James knew about you both and decided that if he couldn't have her, no one could."

That seemed to be a common theme in some of the romantic suspense books I'd read. Of course, Daniel could have thought the same thing.

He shook his head. "Lara claimed James was in the dark, but I think he knew. But I loved Lara and wanted what was best for her. I won't lie. Her inability to choose between us depressed me. I just wanted her to finally pick, so I could move on. The uncertainty was affecting my work."

When he leaned forward, for a few seconds his thoughts were not blocked. What he said had been the truth.

Lara faced me. "Daniel did tell me that he loved me."

"Did you believe him?" I asked her.

"Yes, which made it hard to book the cruise with James. I think my husband could sense I wasn't all that excited about going."

That would point a finger at the husband then. I faced the lawyer. "Did Lara tell you what she did with this rather gruesome photo album?"

"No."

Gavin leaned forward. "How old was this album? Could it have been from say World War II?" He held up a hand. "These type of bizarre images could have been a result of the Nazis doing experiments on people."

He shook his head. "No, it was definitely in modern times, but I didn't study the images closely enough to determine what year they might have been taken."

"Did you recognize any landmarks? I'm wondering if the pictures were of people from Netwood."

Mr. Weintraub glanced to the side. "Yes. I remember

someone standing in front of our library, but I didn't know this person."

"Lara, do you have anything to add?" I didn't ask Bella.

"No. I'm hoping I confided in Cameron, but I often talked to my nail tech, Becca, about a lot of things. She's into the occult, so maybe I told her."

I nodded. "Final question, Mr. Weintraub. What is your take on whether someone ran her off the road or if she lost control due to the road conditions?"

"Lara was a careful driver. I don't remember her texting while driving."

That didn't answer the question. "According to her, she didn't even have her phone with her that night. She said her battery had died."

"That was Lara, all right. She was always forgetting to charge it." His breaths increased and his chin trembled. "What I wouldn't give to talk to her even one more time."

"I imagine everyone wishes they could summon their ancestors like that. I lost my dad last year, yet he's never come to me. Or should I say, if he has, I haven't been able to see him."

"That's too bad."

"Thanks. I know I said last question, but something just occurred to me. Is there any way Lara would have tried to kill herself?" I'd just asked that when she flew into my face.

"Never. I told you that."

"I had to ask, Lara. Please."

A brief smile lifted his lips. "I trust she denied it?"

"Very much so."

"Lara would never take her own life. She loved people and loved life." He picked up a pen from his desk and twirled it on his fingers. "Look, I don't know how I can help you figure things out, but I'd like to try. If you need some information about anyone, ask me."

His words sounded sincere. "Thank you."

Gavin nodded to me, indicating he couldn't think of anything else to ask. We both stood and thanked Mr. Weintraub.

Even though no one was in the lobby, we didn't say anything until we were outside. Because the temperature had dropped quite a lot in the short time we were in there, I hurried to the car. As soon as I slipped in, I turned toward the ladies. "What are your thoughts?"

Lara looked over at Bella and then back at me. "You did a nice job."

We hadn't done much. "Thank you. I meant, did Mr. Weintraub's comments jog your memory or help you in anyway?"

"He seems to think I was obsessed with that photo album. And he could be right. I just don't know."

Gavin nodded. "I agree with Lara's observation." He glanced at the clock on the dashboard. "We are due to her brother's place shortly. Lara can you guide us there?"

"Sure."

Her brother lived about fifteen minutes away in an adjacent town. His home was a modest one-story brick structure situated on several acres of land.

"Does Cameron have any children?" I didn't think it would help with Lara's case, but I liked to know the background of the people we would be speaking with.

"No. He never married, but he was engaged for a few years. He broke up with her shortly before my accident. It's been a hard year for him."

"I can only imagine. I just hope he's come to grips with you actually being with us in spirit."

"Me too."

Cameron answered on the first knock. "Come in." He looked behind us. "Is Lara here?"

That was cute. "Yes."

"Please have a seat. I've been giving everything you told me a lot of thought."

That sounded promising. Gavin and I sat on the sofa while Lara moved next to her brother. Maybe she thought that since they were so close, he'd be able to feel her.

"Tell us what you figured out," I said.

"When I spoke with James about Lara's death, he was understandably quite upset. I didn't know whether it was an act for my sake or if he was truly distraught," Cameron said.

"An act," Lara insisted.

I didn't comment on that.

"Did he describe what happened?" I asked.

"Just that she ran off the road, hit a tree, and died instantly."

"He was fine with that? I mean, was he certain that it had been Lara's fault?"

"I think so," Cameron said. "James spoke with the sheriff, but all Schlemmer would say was that the roads were slippery that night."

"Did a forensic team investigate?" Gavin asked.

Cameron huffed. "Netwood wouldn't spring for something like that unless it was obvious a crime had been committed. "

"See?" Lara said. "The sheriff didn't bother investigating."

"It might be impossible to prove that Lara was run off the road, but for the sake of argument, let's assume she was and go from there." After a few days, if we were at a dead end, we'd have to admit defeat and return home.

"Thank you," Cameron said.

"We've spoken to her friend Karen as well as to her lawyer, Daniel Weintraub."

"You mean my sister's boyfriend."

I'm glad he was aware of their relationship. "Yes. Both

mentioned an album that Lara had found at James' father's house. Did she show it to you?"

"Yes, in fact she asked that I keep it safe."

My pulse shot up. "May we see it? This could be the clue we were hoping for."

"Sure. Let me get it for you."

I smiled and mentally pumped a fist.

chapter nine

CAMERON RETURNED CARRYING a photo album and handed it to me. "Let me warn you, it's disturbing."

"We've seen worse." I explained that Gavin's mom was a medical examiner and that Gavin was studying to be a doctor.

Both Bella and Lara floated toward us and looked over our shoulders. Even though I'd been around them for a while, it was a bit uncomfortable having them so close, but it was Lara's album.

We flipped through the pages and noted that some wounds were more severe than others. "What do you think, Gavin?"

"I don't think you want to know."

What I wouldn't give to be able to communicate telepathically with him. "Tell me."

He looked from me to Cameron and then back to me. "It will sound stupid. Except that you know Lorenzo."

Bingo! "So you agree with Lara that these might be vampire bites?"

"I can't know for sure, but if vampires exist, then maybe."

I turned back to Cameron. "Have you ever heard of people around here discussing vampires?"

He huffed. "No. Even if they had, I wouldn't have listened. I'm a man of science. That being said, there is always a lot of talk of aliens."

I didn't think that would apply to Lara's case.

"May I take a picture of some of these images?" Gavin asked. "As Rihanna mentioned, my mom is a medical examiner. She might be able to shed some light on this."

"Of course. Take as many as you like."

Gavin snapped five photos and then sent them to his mom. He faced me. "Since these people are alive at the time of the shot, she might not be the best person to know about the wound, but it's worth a try."

"I wish Lorenzo were here," I said. "Bella, when you went back to see your dad, you said you and Lorenzo crossed paths, right?"

"Yeah, a few times, but he was not in a good head space."

I swallowed a laugh. I honestly never considered ghosts as having a *head space* before. "Did he say why?"

"He was looking for his coffin, but apparently someone moved it."

"Someone moved it? Why?"

She shrugged. "That's what he wanted to know."

Gavin placed a hand on my wrist. "Do you think we could ask Lorenzo to come here, Bella? His expertise would be useful."

"Who is this Lorenzo person?" Cameron asked. He'd been patient while we had the discussion.

My explanation might convince him that we were all crazy, but I had to give it a try. "This will be hard to believe, but during the cruise you were on, my roommate was murdered."

His mouth dropped open. "I'm sorry. I didn't hear anything about it."

"The captain wanted it that way. A member of the crew killed her. Anyway, somehow, a vampire from New Orleans who died one hundred years ago was freed from his coffin and heard about Bella's death. Since he was a good friend of her great-great-grandmother's, he wanted to help."

That was a really bad summary, but it would have taken too long to explain it properly.

"It's hard enough to come to grips with the idea that ghosts exist let alone vampires." He sighed and then snapped his fingers. "I remember now that when Lara looked at the pictures, she kind of joked and said it looked like they were pictures of people who'd been bitten by vampires."

That was what she told her friend, Karen. "Did either of you know any of these people in the album? It would be great if we could meet with them." I was speaking, of course, to both Cameron and Lara.

Cameron shook his head. "I'm not from Netwood, but I bet either James or the sheriff would know who they are."

I had the sense that the sheriff wouldn't tell us anything, and I actually trusted Mr. Weintraub more than James.

"James would lie," Lara blurted.

That kind of creeped me out having someone read my mind—assuming she had.

"I see. We'll ask around." Just as I was about to say that I wasn't surprised at her comment about James, my stomach grumbled. "We should get going. We don't want to take up too much of your time."

"Not at all. I want to help," Cameron said.

That was good to hear. I smiled and then stood. "We will be in touch, but if you think of anything Lara said or did, please contact us." I gave him my phone number and my email address.

When we left, I suggested we do take out.

Gavin looked over at me. "That's not your style."

"I know, but we have a lot to discuss. For starters, we need to find a way to contact Lorenzo."

"I could go back to New Orleans and try to find him," Bella said.

"Where would you look? Do ghosts have ghost bars where they hang out or something?"

She cracked up. "No, but I wish they did. We just kind of float around and hope to find the person. It's not like we live in houses, you know."

Lara nodded. "That's what I do. I can move really fast when need be and check out places, so finding people isn't too hard. Not only that, I can sense another ghost."

"I had wondered about that. Is that how you and Bella connected?" I wasn't sure that was the right word.

"Actually, Bella recognized my name and came up to me. I was a bit surprised that a stranger knew me."

I could only imagine. "Lara, since we'd like to pick your brain after we eat, how about if Bella goes to New Orleans alone?"

She groaned. "Since it will take you a little time to eat, maybe I can keep Bella company, for say, an hour?" Poor thing sounded so hopeful.

"Sure, but don't be late."

"Don't worry." With that, they disappeared.

"Do you still want to do a drive thru?" Gavin asked.

We were on a time crunch. "Yes."

After we picked up the food, we hurried back to the hotel to brainstorm. I had no idea how long it would take Bella to find Lorenzo, assuming she could, but I hoped Lara would return sooner rather than later.

We spread out our meal on the small table in the room and chowed down.

"What information do you think Lorenzo can help with?" Gavin asked.

"I know he had performance issues, as he called it, because his teeth wouldn't extend. While he never bit anyone, he should be able to recognize if the marks belonged to a vampire."

Gavin drank his soda. "I never was one to follow all the vampire stuff. I figured it was fantasy, and mostly women liked it, but aren't those who are bitten die?"

"I don't think all of them do, but I don't recall ever asking Lorenzo that question. Clearly, the people in these pictures are quite alive."

"True. From what I remember from a television show I watched—like one episode—if a person is bitten by a vampire, they become a vampire—which makes them kind of dead."

I had to think back to the lore. "I think that's true."

"There were at least fifty photos in that book. Do you think it's possible that all of those people are now vampires?"

I shivered at that thought. "I hope not. If that were the case, the whole town would be made up of vampires in no time."

Gavin's phone pinged, and he retrieved it from his pocket. "Good. My mom answered my text."

I leaned over. "What does she say?"

He read it over. "She wasn't much help. Because she doesn't believe in vampires, she thinks it's as if someone is trying to scare a lot of people into thinking vampires exist."

That sounded logical. "Does your mom think that the marks are bite marks, though?"

"She never makes absolute statements, especially after seeing a picture. Someone could have doctored it, but she said if she had to guess, the marks looked like your basic puncture wounds. Mom didn't speculate what kind of instrument was used though."

"The people in these pictures would have to know whether someone stabbed or bit them, right? Or could they have been hypnotized—like Lorenzo was able to do to me—and they just woke up with the marks on their necks?"

"We answer that question, and we might have an idea what we are dealing with."

Gavin was very logical. I gathered the trash from our finished meal and placed it in the bin. Just as I turned around, three ghosts appeared in our room, one of whom was Lorenzo Bambini III.

"Lorenzo! So good to see you." I was sincerely happy to see the vampire ghost—case or no case. He was just a cool guy.

He made a small bow. Like when I first met him, he was wearing his same top hat and dapper suit that was marred by the wooden stake sticking out of his chest.

"You, too, Rihanna." He faced Gavin. "Can this young man see me?"

Gavin smiled. "I can. I've been given the great gift of ghost sight."

"Spectacular." Lorenzo turned back toward me. "Our two ladies briefly told me there was a possible vampire sighting?"

"Kind of." I explained about the album that Lara found in her father-in-law's attic. "Gavin, can you show Lorenzo the pictures?'

"Sure." Gavin held up his phone, slowly scrolling through the few photos he'd taken.

"Does that look like vampire marks to you?" I asked.

His shoulders appeared to droop. "Yes, I'm afraid so. Thankfully, we didn't have as many victims in New Orleans, as Bella said were in the book. If the people were dead, I could speak with them, but clearly they are quite alive."

"I'm glad they are."

He nodded. "I understand."

"I have a question. When a vampire bites a human, do they turn into a vampire?" I asked.

Lorenzo floated over to the bed and appeared to lie down. I say, appeared to, because he was hovering slightly above the comforter.

"It's complicated. As I have explained, I've never bitten anyone, but my blood is vampiric, which is why I'm a vampire. I wasn't a human at one time and then was bitten. My parents were responsible for my condition."

"I see." Though that didn't answer my question. "Let's suppose your brother Alexander bit a person. Would the victim die, live, turn into a vampire, or remain human like before?"

"Again, it's complicated." He kind of sat up. "Here's how it works. From what I've been told, we vampires have a venom in our fangs that contains a kind of sedative. Imagine my brother Alexander hypnotizes this person and then bites him. Supposedly, the person doesn't feel much. I imagine it would be more like a tiny bug bite."

I looked over at Gavin. He'd understand the chemistry of the sedative better than me.

"Are you saying, a person might not be aware they were bitten until they saw the wound the next time they looked in the mirror?" Gavin asked.

"I believe so. It's not like they come back and tell us. I dare say they aren't even aware of much."

"It's like when you hypnotized Rihanna on the boat and had her do that stupid thing, and yet she had no idea she did it," Bella said.

I didn't need Gavin to hear about that. "So you're saying that the person might be unaware she'd even met you, right?"

"Well, all the women know when they've met the great Lorenzo Bambini III."

That was rather egotistical, but I decided not to call him out on it. Maybe when he was alive, he was even more charming.

"I have a question," Gavin said. "Would the person automatically turn into a vampire because they had the vampire DNA in them?"

Lorenzo glanced from Gavin to me. "What is he talking about?"

"You mean about DNA?" He nodded. "I'm not sure when it was discovered, but that part doesn't really matter. Tell us how a person can turn into a vampire. Or can't that happen?" I might have watched too many movies where that occurred.

"It's a process. Again from what I've been told, the human that was bitten first needs to feed on the blood of the vampire who bit them in order to start the process of being turned."

Bella moved to the end of the bed and faced Lorenzo. "If this person was unaware they were bitten, why would they think to bite some vampire? In fact, how would you even go about finding a vampire?"

Lorenzo smiled. "Many vampires want to turn humans in order to grow our population. Once they bite their victim, they often stay around and taunt them into biting them back. It's like waving a bottle of liquor in front of an alcoholic."

"Or waving something red in front of a bull," I threw in.

"Exactly."

Gavin stood and then paced. "Let me get this straight. When a human is bitten, they will remain human as long as they don't feed on more blood?"

"Yes, and the urge goes away in a few days." Lorenzo lifted a wispy hand. "I forgot one step. After they drink from the donor vampire blood, they need to drink human blood."

"Yuk," Lara said. "Dare I say very few people go with this option?"

"More than you think. The need for blood is strong."

I had to think about this. "If all of this is true, how does Lara fit into the scheme of things? She wasn't bitten."

Bella smiled. "I think Lara uncovered a deep dark secret and someone wanted to shut her up."

"You might be right, but what proof do we have?" I asked her.

"Ah, duh. Lara is dead. Murdered in fact, if we believe her."

"Would James know if there was a connection?" Gavin asked.

"Maybe, but who's to say he's not involved? After all, the album came from his dad's attic," Lara said.

"Involved in what exactly is the key to the case," I said.

chapter ten

"**LORENZO,** do you have any idea why someone would have an album full of people who'd been bitten?"

"*Moi?* Why would I?" He waved a hand. "Actually, I do know. It's an album of trophies if you will."

Both Gavin and I stared at Lorenzo. "Trophies? As in James' father was a vampire, and these are his victims?" That was ridiculous.

Lorenzo lifted his head. "My brother has such an album. I saw it recently in fact. In my day, we didn't have those fancy phone cameras you young folk have now. It wasn't like we could carry around a big clunky camera in case we got lucky and bit someone either."

"I suppose not." But why didn't he mention this before? Ugh. I needed to remember that ghosts had a tendency to withhold information. "Remind me never to meet this brother. He's like a serial killer."

Lorenzo sighed as he shook his head. "Not in the least. He doesn't kill those he bites, though he could. We Bambinis are a higher class than that."

"I had no idea there were so many different types of

vampires." And yes, I was kind of being sarcastic. I think being around Bella was rubbing off on me.

"Like I explained on the boat, some vampire families have integrated with humans, which is why my family can handle sunlight."

That wasn't what I was referring to when I said there were different kinds. I meant there seemed to be many class distinctions in the vampire realm.

Lara moved closer to Lorenzo. "Is there any advantage to being a vampire?"

"Oh, my yes. We live a long time—or rather until someone decides to kill us, assuming we aren't a member of one of those rare families who are immortal." He tried to rub his chin. "To be honest, living forever doesn't appeal to me anymore."

I didn't think I'd want to live forever either. I liked that each day was a gift. I'm sure if I ever spoke to my dad again, even he'd agree.

"Do you think we should try to find out why James' dad had this album in the first place?" Gavin asked. "We can't assume he was a vampire. And if he were, no one would admit it."

I loved how Gavin kept us on track.

"I think we should find out who these people are," Lara said. "Then you can ask them what happened."

"Gavin, can you show the pictures to Lara? She might recognize a few of them."

He pulled out his phone, and on the second picture, she sucked in a breath. "That's Caitlyn Shorter."

I immediately took out my phone and jotted down the name. "Did you know her well?"

"Yes, quite well, but we lost track of each other once she moved away from Netwood."

That was disappointing. "When did she move?"

Lara didn't answer for a moment. "In December. Her

mom became ill, and Caitlyn and the family moved farther west to be with her."

Convenient timing. "Okay, how about the next one?"

Gavin flipped to the third photo.

"That's Christine Darden. She passed away last October. I think her family said it was due to a heart problem."

I noted the name. Let's hope we could speak to at least one of these possible victims. "Next?"

Lara shook her head. "I don't know him. We are a small town, but that doesn't mean I know everyone." She didn't know the final one either.

"Maybe Mr. Weintraub knows them," Bella suggested.

"Lara, do you trust Daniel?" I asked.

"I do. Go ahead and ask him," Lara said.

Gavin swiped off his phone. "How about you three let us get some sleep? Tomorrow is a new day."

Bella floated to the door. "Come on. That's code for them wanting privacy."

I chuckled. Bella had learned well. "What will you three be doing? Remember, if you chat outside the doorway, we can hear you."

"And we can hear you!" Bella grinned.

"Fine, so how about haunting someplace else?"

Lorenzo turned to Lara. "Perhaps, dear lady, you would be so kind as to give me a tour of your town."

She smiled. "I'd be happy to."

I guess being dead wasn't so bad after all. "Bye!" I said.

Once the three slipped through the wall, Gavin came over to me. "I need a hug. This ghost stuff is a bit overwhelming but exciting at the same time."

"I hear you." I opened my arms and enjoyed his warmth and love.

Gavin and I were up fairly early the next morning and headed down the street to the diner where we'd eaten before. Where our ghost friends were, I didn't know. Hopefully, they were spying on someone useful.

To my delight, Stella, the same waitress who served us yesterday, was there and came over.

"Hello, you two. I'm glad to see you're back."

I smiled. "Can't beat good food and good service."

"You sure can't." She handed us the menus. "Coffee?"

"Yes, please."

As soon as she left, I had an idea. "How about showing Stella the images of the people Lara couldn't identify? She might be able to shed some light on things."

"Sure."

The album seemed to have more females than males, but maybe that meant there were more male vampires. I leaned back in my seat. "Are we crazy?"

Gavin's eyes widened. "For what?"

"For thinking vampires have infiltrated Netwood, Nebraska? There has to be another explanation."

"Try me."

"I wish I had another one. It's why we need to find these *victims*, as Lorenzo called them, and talk to them."

"I agree."

Stella carried over our coffee and then took our order. "Stella, we're looking to speak to a few people. I was hoping you might know them."

Gavin showed her the photos. She looked through each one. "I know Kathy Dumont and Phil Eastwick."

I wrote down their names. They were number four and five. "Do they live in town?"

"They did."

Oh, come on. This was beginning to be a little creepy. "What happened to them?"

"Kathy was transferred out west, and Phil retired to Florida."

"When was this?" I asked.

She shrugged. "Late last year, I think."

"Thanks." Stella didn't seem to know more than that. At least she had an open mind so I could tell she was being truthful.

No sooner had she left to fill our order when a man in uniform came in. He was in his mid-thirties, I'd say, and quite fit. When he passed our booth, I spotted the name Sheriff Schlemmer on his name tag. What do you know?

I covered the side of my mouth so that the sheriff wouldn't hear me—or read my lips. "We should ask him about these people."

"Why? It's not like they're missing."

"Neither Lara nor Stella knew the name of the first person listed. Maybe she is missing."

Gavin blew on his coffee and then sipped the drink. "You are tenacious."

"If you had a sick person in your care, you'd do everything possible to find the cause of their illness."

"You're right." He handed me his phone. "Ask him."

It would seem less threatening if only one of us approached the man. Before the sheriff was swamped with other people complaining about some wrong doing—and before I lost my courage—I took the phone with the image of the remaining unidentified person and walked the ten feet to where the sheriff was sitting by himself in a booth.

"Excuse me, sheriff." I said that in the sweetest, most innocent, tone I could muster. And trust me, I had to dig deep for the super sweet part. Yeah, and the innocent part, too.

He looked up. "May I help you?"

I held out the picture of the woman. "Do you know who she is?"

While he hadn't put up any mental barriers as I approached, he shut me out real fast when he saw the photo.

"No, why?"

I could from the way he lowered his eyes, that he'd lied. "How long have you been sheriff here?"

"Excuse me? Who are you?"

"A friend of someone who died."

"Let me guess. Lara Finley." His jaw hardened. "Let me tell you something, little lady. You have no idea what you are dealing with. I suggest you go back to where you came from—and quick."

That was rather threatening. He was lucky I didn't summon my two gargoyle shifter friends here. They'd extract the information out of the sheriff. "Sure thing. Thanks for all your *help*."

I know that sarcasm is not good, but it was my default attitude of late. I spun around and headed back to Gavin certain the sheriff knew exactly who the person was and why I was asking about her.

I handed Gavin his phone. Since I wasn't bubbling over with enthusiasm, he probably figured that things hadn't gone well. Our food had been delivered while I was having my *wonderful* conversation with the sheriff.

"No name?" he asked.

"No, though the sheriff knew her. I'll tell you later." I dug into my meal.

For the most part, we ate in silence. When we finished, we waved to Stella for our bill. As quickly as we could, we paid and left.

The moment I stepped outside, refreshing air rushed into my lungs.

"What happened?" Gavin asked.

I told him. "The fact he practically threatened me implies there is something here."

"Maybe you can ask Jaxson to do a bit of research on these people. If he can get an email address or a phone number, we can contact them."

Tension flowed out of me at his suggestion. "That's a great idea."

He flashed me a smile as we headed back to the hotel. I wasn't surprised when I found our three beings there.

Bella was smiling. "Guess what we learned?"

I was thrilled they'd been successful at gathering more information, since we had only learned the names of two more people from our list. Too bad none of them were in town. "Do tell."

"The sheriff received a phone call," Bella said.

"Do you know who it was from?"

"No, but he was not happy."

That had me interested. I sat on the bed. "What exactly did he say?"

Bella looked over at Lara. "It was hard to tell," Lara said. "I tried to listen in, but he had the phone pressed to his ear."

"But you heard his side of the conversation, right?"

"Yes. The sheriff asked if anyone was hurt. I couldn't tell what the answer was. He told the person that they'd have to go on patrol again."

"Interesting."

"Do you want us to keep an eye on the sheriff?" Lorenzo said. "We can tell you where he goes and maybe who he sees, assuming Lara knows them."

"That would be awesome. You don't have to head back to New Orleans? Bella told us you were a bit upset about your missing coffin, not that I blame you."

"Bella is a blabber mouth, I see."

"Losing a coffin is important," she shot back.

"I know, but I'll find it. I think I know who took it."

Not that I planned to be involved in this, but Lorenzo seemed to need to talk about it. "Who?"

"My brother Alexander. He's taken over the family business, and I don't think he wants me to return to my coffin. My youngest brother, Noble, always liked me. I bet he would take the stake out of my chest if he knew where to find me—or rather my body."

"I'm sorry."

"I'll worry about it later. I have all the time in the world to find where I'm buried. I want to help you all. "

"Thank you." I looked around. "Anything else?"

"Maybe we should ask my brother if Gavin can take more pictures of the people in the album," Lara said. "There were a lot in there, and I bet I could identify more of them."

"Great idea. I'll call Cameron and ask if we can stop by later tonight, since he'll be at work now. Because we have some time, why don't you guys see what the sheriff is up to? I'll try to find out about the people we do know."

"Okay." As soon as Lara floated out, the other two followed.

Once they were gone, I pulled up my computer to do a video chat with Jaxson, and hopefully catch up with Glinda—and yes, her adorable familiar, Iggy.

chapter eleven

I HADN'T SPOKEN with Glinda since we'd arrived, and I was anxious to hear what she was up to. A few seconds after I called, she answered. I figured her slight delay was to make sure Iggy was with her.

"Hey, stranger. How is Nebraska?"

"Cold."

Glinda chuckled. "It's a balmy eighty degrees in sunny Florida."

"Way to rub it in." Good thing we'd be home soon.

"I'm glad I didn't go with you then," Iggy said.

"Hey, buddy. You were smart not to come. It's really cold here, and I know you don't do well in that climate." He shook his head, looking way too human. "Other than enjoying the weather, how are things going there?" I asked Glinda, not quite ready to delve into our problems.

"Good. Jaxson and I have a job, but it's just spying on two sixteen-year-olds. The parents don't trust them."

"You should ask Hugo and Genevieve to watch them. I bet they'd like that." Considering those two didn't need to eat or sleep, the kids would be well supervised.

"We think alike," Glinda said. "They are watching over them and are very happy to have something to do."

"I bet."

"How is the search for Lara's killer coming?" Glinda asked.

Iggy perked up, and I was glad of it. He often had good insights. "We need some help."

"I can help," Iggy said.

"Great." I had no idea what he could do though. "I am sending Jaxson the names and photos of a few people—with hopefully more to come—who might be connected to Lara's death."

Glinda called Jaxson over, and once he joined us, I detailed what we'd uncovered.

"You think these people were victims of vampire attacks?" Jaxson asked. "And that Lara found out so someone killed her?"

"It's a theory." Normally, Glinda's fiancé was quite open minded, but I understood why he was skeptical, despite me and a few others telling him about Lorenzo. "The thing that struck me as odd, is that none of the people are still in town. I'd like to know why they left. Did they fear being attacked again? Hearing from them about what happened would be helpful."

"Did you ask Gavin's mom about the marks?" Glinda asked.

"I did, but she couldn't give a definitive answer."

"Send me the information," Jaxson said. "I'll get right on it."

"Thank you." It took only a few seconds to email him the images and the names.

"Can we help with anything else?" Glinda asked.

"I'm not sure. While Lorenzo has been answering our

questions about vampires, I don't think Bella, Lara, or Lorenzo are experts in being ghosts."

"What are you wondering about?" Glinda asked. "Not that I know all that much either."

"Have you ever met a ghost who has lost his or her memory?"

She looked off to the side. "I've had ghosts who have remembered the time of their death being very different from what actually happened."

"Darn. I was afraid of that."

I could have spent hours chatting with Glinda about the occult, but Gavin and I had work to do, especially since our time in Nebraska was limited. "Email me anything you find out about those people. We're hoping we can learn the names of more victims. I can't imagine every one of those who were bitten—if that's what happened—left town."

Jaxson's phone dinged, indicating my message had arrived. He opened the file and showed Glinda. "Interesting," she said.

"What?"

"These aren't selfies."

I hadn't thought of that. "What are you saying? That someone lined up these people and took their picture?"

"Maybe."

That gave me an idea. "I'll see if when I look at the rest of the pictures, whether or not the background gives us a clue where some of the photos were taken. Daniel pointed out that one person was in front of the Netwood library."

"Good thinking, and let us know," Glinda said.

"I have a sweater I can wear if you really need me," Iggy said.

I smiled, remembering all of the outfits Aunt Fern had made for him for Christmas presents. "I'll keep that in mind, Iggy." I glanced over at Gavin and then back at my cousin. "I need to go."

"Keep in touch," my cousin said.

"Will do."

When I disconnected, I felt a bit more grounded.

"Jaxson's going to help, I hear," Gavin said.

"Yes, but we really need to speak to these *vampire* victims."

Gavin moved next to me on the bed. "What if the album has nothing to do with Lara's death?"

"Meaning?"

"Meaning that James could have run Lara off the road for the reason we stated—he sensed her heart wasn't into their marriage anymore."

"That's what divorce is for, but that does open up a whole slew of other options. To be fair, we should ask Daniel Weintraub if one of his lady friends might have decided that Lara needed to go."

He nodded. "See? We can't be so focused on one thing that we overlook something else."

Gavin was right. "I know we want to speak with Cameron again, but in the meantime, maybe we should pick Lara's nail tech's brain."

"Do you really think Lara would have told her about the album though?"

"Maybe, especially since her nail tech is into the occult. In the meantime, we should send that last image to Daniel Weintraub to see if he can identify her."

"I can do that."

"Thanks. Besides, I need Lara to tell me where she had her nails done."

"There is that."

"Who else should we be focusing on?" I asked. "James doesn't think his wife was murdered, though her brother and Daniel believe she was."

Gavin looked off to the side. "This is why I want to be a doctor. It seems more cut and dried."

I chuckled. "Really? People come in with a myriad of symptoms, and you have to narrow it down. That's what we're doing."

He smiled. "You're telling me that by helping with the case, I'll be honing my doctoring skills?"

That might have been a stretch, but it was possible. "Yes."

No sooner had Gavin emailed the last picture to Daniel Weintraub than our three cohorts floated in.

"You won't believe what the sheriff is doing," Bella said.

"Looking for criminals?" That's what lawmen were supposed to do.

"Kind of." Bella smiled.

I looked over at Lorenzo who was usually a bit more forthcoming than Bella. He slightly bowed his head. "The sheriff is searching for vampires."

If I had been drinking something, I would have sprayed it everywhere. "What? How do you know that?"

Lara floated in front of me. "We don't know that exactly, but I think it's true. I heard him mention Caitlyn Shorter."

"That was one of the women in the album," I said.

"Yes, and apparently, they went in search of the person who might have bitten her."

"Did you hear the sheriff say the word *bite*?" Gavin asked.

All three ghosts nodded.

I looked over at Gavin. "What do you make of it?"

"Beats me."

"Did they find this vampire person?" I asked.

Lorenzo moved in front of us. "Yes. And before you ask if he is indeed a vampire, the answer is yes. I know because I can sense these things, despite being dead. I have to say, I was quite excited to learn I haven't lost all of my powers."

Poor Lorenzo. "You can turn into an animal at will. That's a power you still have."

"There is that. Now if my animal could sniff out the location of my coffin, I'd be a lot happier."

"True."

"Did they arrest this man?" Gavin asked.

"The sheriff brought him in for questioning, but I overheard him talking to someone about how he wasn't sure if he could make the charges stick," Lara said.

That would be a problem. "A normal court wouldn't believe vampires even existed, so that would be an issue. Did you know this other man the sheriff spoke to? He wasn't the deputy, was he?"

"No. I've never seen him before."

"What about the man arrested?" Gavin asked. "Did you know him?"

Lara shook her head. "No. And I do know a fair amount of people in town. I just wish we could use a camera and record what we see."

"That is a limitation of being a ghost," I admitted.

"Tell her about what the sheriff talked about," Bella said.

Lorenzo grunted and then sighed. "It's quite terrible, really. I heard mention of a vampire slayer kit."

"A vampire slayer kit?" I asked. "What exactly is that? I mean, I've seen a lot of movies, but I know real life isn't the same."

Lorenzo faced away from us, as if the topic was too painful to talk about. Bella moved over to him, I guess to provide him some support. I couldn't hear what she said, but he turned toward us and moved closer.

"A vampire slayer kit is what it sounds like. It's meant to kill a vampire. Yes, the kit contains a wooden stake with a hammer, because you know, it does kill our kind. It also has all the usual Hollywood stuff, like a bible, holy water, a cross, some Wolf's Bane, and stuff like that. And, of course, a gun with silver bullets."

"That is very Hollywood." Lorenzo taught me that what we know about vampires isn't necessarily the truth.

"Most definitely," he said. "Most of it is fairly useless, but the vampires aren't going to tell people that. For instance, we don't turn away when someone tosses holy water on us or if they brandish a cross. While the Wolf's Bane is poisonous, we can survive it. As for the gun with silver bullets? I honestly don't know. Not a lot of vampires were killed in my time."

"We know the stake works," I said.

Gavin placed a hand on my shoulder. "Rihanna, while true, do you really see the sheriff driving a stake into a man's heart because he thinks this person might be a vampire?"

"Honestly? No. He wouldn't be able to explain the death."

Bella floated down to the bed. "Who's to say the sheriff has to do it? He might let the man go free and then hire someone to kill this vampire."

That was a terrible thought. "Do you think that Netwood, Nebraska has some underground society full of vampire killers?" I tried not to laugh at my question.

"Most certainly," Lorenzo said with a lot of conviction. "Or maybe I should say probably. I do know that New Orleans has had vampire slayers for centuries."

"Wow. How do we find these vampire killers?" I asked.

"By word of mouth, I suppose. Just so you know, most serious vampire slayer groups make their own *kits*, for lack of a better word. They build their boxes and put their instruments of destruction inside."

"I think I've seen where you can buy them online," Gavin said. "I always figured it was a Halloween gimmick."

"On line?" Lorenzo asked.

Since Lorenzo was killed in 1922, the poor guy had so

much to learn. If he ever did find his coffin and convinced someone to remove his stake, he'd be far behind in our society. I wasn't sure he'd be able to cope—which had been Bella's point when we were on the cruise.

Gavin went over to the desk and retrieved his laptop. "I'll find a picture to show you what I'm talking about." After a few keystrokes, Gavin located a vampire slayer kit. "Is this what you're used to?" he asked Lorenzo.

The vampire floated over. He stared at the screen and then moved behind it. I kept forgetting that he didn't have television in his day, though he had seen me video chat with Glinda and Iggy when we were on the yacht, and he'd witnessed his brother taking photos with his cell phone.

"That's incredible," he said, "though not all that effective—other than the stake and possibly the gun."

"What else can you tell us about these vampire slayer groups?" I asked. "Do they meet regularly or only on line? Sorry. Not on line. I forgot that in your day, the Internet didn't exist."

He huffed. "I don't know about Nebraska, but in New Orleans, I've heard they meet in different homes. They don't want to be caught any more than we want them to catch us."

"That makes sense," I chimed in. "Do you have any suggestions on how we can find out who these people are?" I didn't know how Lorenzo would know though.

"Somewhere—whether it is on a window at their home or on their automobile, or even on their horse's saddle—you might see an emblem that shows they are a member of this slayer society."

I couldn't image it would be the same now as that was one hundred years ago. "What did this symbol look like?"

"It was subtle. It is a red circle with a cross in the middle with a red drop of what we assumed was blood somewhere in the image. It's approximately two inches in diameter, so you have to know what you're looking for."

Bella kind of snapped her fingers—or should I say, she attempted to. Then she grunted. It was almost as if these three kept forgetting they were dead.

"If Lara found an album in her father-in-law's attic, maybe there is a vampire kit there too," Bella said.

"I'm not sure what good it will do to know that her father-in-law was a vampire slayer, but it might imply James is one now," I said.

Lara seemed to float to the ground. "Does that mean he might have killed me?"

chapter twelve

"LARA, you can't draw that conclusion," Gavin said. "There is no evidence that your husband tried to kill you. That being said, I do think we should look into him a bit more."

"I agree with Gavin," I said. "Why don't you guys check out her father-in-law's attic to see if maybe there is a vampire slayer kit there—or perhaps other photo albums."

"It's been over a month since I died. I'm not sure what James has done with the place. The house could be sold by now for all I know."

That could be a problem. "It won't take long to look, right?"

"No. We'll check it out. Be back in a flash," Lara said.

And then they were gone. "Darn, I forgot to ask about the nail tech."

"I think we'll have more success taking another look at the album that Cameron has," Gavin said.

I stilled. "We have to be careful not to tell anyone where we saw those pictures, or Cameron might be in danger—assuming that was what caused someone to run Lara off the road in the first place." I hissed in a breath. "Did I tell Stella that Lara's brother had the album?"

"I don't recall." Gavin stood and paced the small room. "What do you think of asking Hugo to stand watch over him? I think Cameron needs protection a lot more than those two teenagers do."

"I agree, but I won't do it if Glinda really needs him."

"She has Genevieve. Do they really need two gargoyle shifters to keep watch?"

I didn't know what their father or fathers thought they were doing. "Let me ask her."

I called Glinda again via video chat, and she answered right away.

"What's wrong?" Glinda asked.

I explained that Cameron might be in danger. "Could you possibly spare Hugo to watch over him?"

"Sure, no problem. The kids' dad thinks they are into some bad stuff, but Genevieve can handle it. Of course, we'll call the sheriff if we find out they are doing anything illegal."

"Great." I gave her the address of the hotel. "I hope Hugo can find it."

Glinda stilled. "Me too. Uh-oh. How will you be able to communicate with him?"

"Darn. I forgot he can't talk." Iggy was on the sofa next to Glinda. "Do you think you can lend us Iggy for a couple of days?"

Iggy waddled over. "Just so you know, I now charge for my services."

I almost cracked up. "What kind of compensation are you looking for, young man?"

"A flower a day for a month."

It was what Iggy loved to eat. "Deal."

He looked over at Glinda. "Do you know where my warm clothes are?"

"They are in my closet back at the apartment."

"Chop, chop. Go get them."

Glinda looked over at me. "I think I'll send Genevieve instead. Iggy doesn't deserve to go." She winked.

"I agree. Talking back to you and demanding things is unacceptable behavior."

He dropped onto his stomach. "Fine. I'm sorry. Would you *please* find my clothes for me—and my heating pad?"

Glinda smiled. "That's better. Let me check with Genevieve first to see if she's okay with letting Hugo go off on his own. Rihanna, I'll call you back."

"Thank you." We disconnected, and then I glanced over at Gavin who looked like he'd seen another ghost. "What's wrong?"

I hope someone else hadn't shown up uninvited. A quick glance confirmed we were the only ones there.

"Who was with Glinda?"

Gavin had been on his computer, so he hadn't seen who it was. "Iggy, why?"

"I...ah...heard him. Is that possible?"

I grinned. "That's amazing! I'm guessing the spell Levy's coven performed worked for not only ghosts but for familiars too. Who knew?"

He blew out a breath. "I have to say, this new development will make things easier when I see him."

"For sure." I hoped Gavin was ready for Iggy's sassy comments. "You probably heard that Hugo might be here shortly. If he comes, should we tell Cameron that we are providing a gargoyle-shifting bodyguard?"

"You said Hugo can cloak himself without much trouble, so maybe not."

I nodded. "You're probably right. Cameron might act strangely if he knew he was being watched. Hugo's rather stiff appearance, along with the fact he doesn't talk, could be unsettling."

Gavin smiled. "Even I'm still a little creeped out by him."

"Iggy will be with us, but if Hugo needs to tell us something, he can teleport back instantly."

"I like that plan, but Iggy won't be happy if we are walking everywhere."

"Since iguanas are cold-blooded, he can stay in the room. If he's wearing an outfit, the maids will think he's a pet and not bother him."

"Or tell him to cloak himself if anyone comes in."

My boyfriend was smart. "Good idea."

Before we could come up with the next step in our plan, the three ghosts flew through the wall. "We found nothing," Lara announced.

"Nothing, as in nothing of use, or nothing as in as the attic totally empty?"

"Totally empty," she said.

"There was a For Sale sign on the front lawn," Bella added. She looked over at Lara. "What would your husband have done with his father's stuff?"

That was a good question.

"James was kind of a cheapskate pack rat. I bet he sold what he could and found space in our basement or attic for the rest." Her eyes widened. "We should look there."

"That's a good—" And they were off. Those three seemed to be able to communicate telepathically. "Idea."

Since it was Lara's death we were investigating, it made sense that she'd be in charge of the investigation—or at least the ghostly part.

Less than five minutes after the three of them disappeared, Hugo showed up with Iggy in his grasp, and my heart soared. I was so happy to see him. "Iggy!!"

"Hey." He looked around. "I don't think I'll get used to this teleporting stuff."

I didn't know why. He'd been moved about quite often. "Thankfully, you're here in one piece." I looked over at Hugo. "Thank you."

He nodded.

Gavin stepped up to them. "Hi, Iggy."

Iggy looked at me. "Now, he says something to me?"

"Yes, it's because Levy's spell allowed him to see not only ghosts, but to hear you too."

"Is that so?" He looked back at Gavin. "So, what are your intentions toward Rihanna."

My mouth opened. I so wanted to strangle the little bugger. "Iggy Goodall, that is none of your business."

Gavin grinned. "I assure you, that my intentions are quite honorable."

"They better be. If you mess with Rihanna in any way, I'll sic Hugo on you."

Gavin laughed and held up his palms. "Oh, no. Anything but that."

"Okay, okay. Enough," I said. "It is nice that I don't have to translate anymore."

Iggy lifted a claw. "There is that." He faced Hugo and then turned back to us. "Hugo wants to know where he can find this Cameron person."

We were back to business, I see. "Give me a sec."

I located the address of Cameron's office, and described how to get there the best I could, though Hugo wouldn't be using roads. I further explained that Hugo needed to stay cloaked. "Cameron will be better off if he has no idea that you're there."

Hugo nodded. "Should I go with Hugo?" Iggy asked.

"It's cold outside. I think you're better off here where you can help us brainstorm." To be honest, I had no idea if Iggy would be outside at all. I just wanted Iggy to be safe.

Iggy looked up at his friend. "Maybe tomorrow."

Hugo handed Iggy to me and then took off. Despite my instructions, I would have thought he'd want to see a map, but he and Genevieve did find me in the middle of the ocean last month so perhaps gargoyle shifters had a built in map in their heads. After witnessing what Hugo was able to do on other cases, I wouldn't put anything past him.

I gave Iggy a quick kiss even though I was well aware he didn't like a lot of affection. "I'm really happy to see you."

"I know," Iggy said with a lot of confidence.

Glinda's familiar didn't seem to have a humble bone in his body. "Where is your heating pad?"

"Uh-oh."

"If you need it, maybe Hugo can teleport back and pick it up for you."

"Maybe later. The room temperature in here is okay for now."

I smiled. "I'm glad."

"What do you need help with?" Iggy asked.

"I wish I knew." I proceeded to fill him in on what we'd recently learned.

"Will I be able to meet Lorenzo in person?"

I wasn't sure why Iggy seemed so fascinated with him. "Of course, but remember, even when he was alive, he wasn't the biting kind of vampire."

"I know, but even if he did bite, I don't think I have the kind of blood he needs."

I laughed. "That's probably true."

For a good thirty minutes, we discussed our options for solving this case. Because we couldn't visit Cameron until he finished work—which would be in a few hours—we batted around why someone might have wanted Lara dead. The vampire theory seemed to be our number one choice.

I checked the time. "I wonder what's taking our friends so long?"

"James might have a big house. It can't be easy searching through his stuff, especially if it is in boxes. Remember, our ghosts can't open anything," Gavin said.

I dropped back onto the bed. "I forgot about that. I'd suggest we ask James to help us, but he could have been the one to harm his wife."

"Agreed. We certainly don't need to tip anyone off that we might have figured out why Lara was murdered."

My mind spun. It was so frustrating having so many unanswered questions.

Eventually, the three wanderers showed up. "You guys took your sweet time." As soon as I said that, I regretted my comment. I didn't like whiny people and never wanted to be one.

"Better late than staked," Lorenzo said with some joy.

"What does that mean? Did you find another staked vampire?" I was kidding, but perhaps he wasn't.

"No. It rhymed. That's all."

Iggy crawled over to me. "Is that him?"

I smiled. "Everyone, this is Iggy. Bella has met him, but not you two."

Lara floated over to him. "Nice to meet you."

He studied her for a moment. "You look nice."

That comment surprised me considering Lara's damaged face, but I was very happy Iggy didn't call attention to her injuries.

"Thank you."

Iggy then turned his attention to Lorenzo. "Are you a real vampire?"

Lorenzo bowed. "As real as they come—or shall I say, when I was alive, I had vampire blood coursing through my veins."

I didn't need Iggy to ask any embarrassing questions about biting people since Lorenzo had an issue in that department. "What did you find at James' house?" I asked.

"Nothing, mostly because we couldn't open any boxes. It was quite maddening," Lorenzo said.

I could only imagine. "So you didn't see any vampire slayer boxes or more photo albums lying about?"

"No." Lorenzo stood taller. "I think something's there though. I felt it, but I can't say exactly what *it* was. If I had to guess, I'd say it was a vampire slayer kit since in the past I've reacted to the Wolf's Bane inside."

How could a dead person be allergic to something? I'd ask, but I had the feeling he wouldn't know, especially since the Wolf Bane I knew came in a bottle—a closed one.

"If we need to, we can ask Genevieve to come here and look through the house," I said. "She can open things."

"Who's Genevieve?" Lara asked.

I forgot that Lara had no idea who the two gargoyle shifters were, so I gave a brief outline of their abilities. "In fact, that's why Iggy is here. Hugo teleported here with him." Plus, I was missing him.

Iggy lifted his head and shook it slightly. "You forgot to say Hugo can only communicate with me."

"Yes. You are right. It's one of the reasons why Iggy needs to be here." I explained that our mute gargoyle shifter was here to protect Cameron.

"My brother's in danger?"

"Hopefully not." I explained my logic.

Lara nodded. "Thank you for asking Hugo to watch over Cameron."

"No problem."

"We need to tell you something," Lara said.

"What is it?"

"There is something bad going on outside of town," Lara said.

"Define bad." We might have a different definition.

"There were a lot of ambulances and police cars about a mile out of the main part of town."

"Was there an accident?" Gavin asked.

"We couldn't tell. We'd just come from my home, but we didn't stop to investigate."

Though if they didn't stop to investigate, and if they couldn't open any boxes, why did it take them so long to look through James' house? I guess some questions would never be answered.

"Since we have nothing to do until Cameron finishes work, how about if Gavin and I grab a quick bite and then see if the sheriff is free to answer some questions about the people in the photos?"

"He didn't answer you before," Gavin reminded me. "And he might be at the accident scene."

"If he is there, I'd love to see if I can do a better job reading his mind."

"Sounds good." Gavin pulled out his phone. "Lara, do you recognize any of the backgrounds in these pictures. They clearly weren't taken by the person in the picture but rather by someone else. I noticed two of them seem to be in the same place."

Since Lara couldn't grab hold of the phone, Gavin slowly panned through the pictures.

She sucked in a breath at the third photo. "That's the local clinic."

Yes! "Where is that?" I asked.

"On Century Avenue and Azele. I can show you where it is."

"Great! We need to eat and should be back in less than an hour. In the meantime, can you guys see what all the fuss is about with the ambulances?" I had the sense that Bella would like to check it out.

"Definitely," Bella said. "Lorenzo, have you ever been inside an ambulance?"

"No."

"I haven't either," Bella said. "But no touching of the equipment." Then Bella laughed.

As soon as they left, I looked over at Iggy. "My purse isn't big enough for you to fit. Besides, since the restaurant is nearby, we will be walking there, and it will be cold."

"Bummer. I'll stay here then."

Poor Iggy. "I'll try to bring something back for you to eat."

"Okay." He sounded a bit dejected, but that couldn't be helped.

Once we put on our warm gear, Gavin and I left. "How about the diner?" I asked. "It will be quick."

"Sure."

The walk over was more pleasant than before. The sun had come out, and the wind was still. We crossed the street, walked three blocks west, and entered the restaurant. The noise level was quite high, and my body tensed from the anxiety floating in the air.

"What's wrong?" Gavin always seemed to know when I was reading a lot of minds at once.

"I can't tell exactly, but I think someone died—someone important to the town."

"Maybe the waitress can tell us."

A server came over. "Sit anywhere. I'll be right over."

Her comment was a bit strained, and she seemed highly upset over something. We found a booth and slid in. "I wonder who passed away."

"I'm sure we'll find out soon enough," Gavin said. "At least I know it's not one of our ghosts or Cameron."

"True, but it's a person everyone seems to know."

The waitress came over, her hands clutching the pad tightly. "Can I get you something to drink?"

"I'd like a coffee." I pretended to glance around. "People seem rather agitated. Did something happen?"

"Yes. It's terrible. The sheriff was murdered."

chapter thirteen

DREAD COURSED THROUGH MY VEINS. "Sheriff Schlemmer was killed? How?"

"We don't know any details, other than he was chasing some criminal and died." The waitress' chin wobbled. "He kept us all safe. This town is going to miss him."

"I bet Deputy Denison is frantic," I said, hoping to wring out more information.

"He's in shock or so someone told me."

Ah yes, the gossip tree. I loved small towns. "I'm sorry for your loss." That was what Glinda would always say. Being the daughter of someone who ran a funeral home, it was ingrained in her brain.

"Thanks." She turned to Gavin. "What would you like to drink?"

"Coffee is fine."

"I'll be right back."

I wasn't all that confident that we would be served quickly as this girl clearly had other things on her mind. I turned back to Gavin. "Now I know what the ambulances that Lara told us about were for."

Gavin nodded. "I had this crazy thought."

"What is it?"

"Could Lara's death and the sheriff's death be related?"

Glinda and I were all for crazy ideas, but this one was really out there. "Based on what evidence? That they're both dead? Or the fact the sheriff arrested a *vampire*?" I mouthed the last word.

"Both maybe? Lara told people about this album full of vampire victims."

I had to think it through. "If the vampires, or those who are aware of them, wanted to keep their existence a secret, that theory has potential."

Gavin waved a hand. "Strike that idea. I forgot that the guy in jail can't be a vampire."

"Why would you say that? Lorenzo said he's one."

"The man was caught in the daytime. Vampires are allergic to the sun."

I had no idea that Gavin was up on his vampire lore. "That's what I thought at first, too, but that's all Hollywood stuff. Remember, Lorenzo mentioned that his family integrated with humans, which is why his family can handle sunlight. Maybe it's the same with this guy."

"Maybe."

"We have to toss out our vampire knowledge. I'm thinking books and movies make that stuff up about vampires and their problem with the sun to increase the conflict in the story and to make the vampires creepier."

"Wow. That puts a new spin on things."

That was the problem. Now we had too many options. "If Lorenzo said the man they brought in for questioning is a vampire, I'm tending to believe him."

"If that's the case, I'd love to have a conversation with this guy."

I chuckled. "Don't tell me you'd ask if he's willing to donate some blood so you can test it?"

His eyebrows rose. "Would that be so bad? We need to understand what these people are capable of."

"According to Lorenzo, vampires can kill, just like humans can kill, but his family never did, or so he believed." I leaned back. "I think your initial thoughts are right. Some friends of this man decided they didn't want the sheriff arresting or even questioning their kind and took justice into their own hands."

Gavin leaned forward. "If a vampire killed a sheriff, that's just asking to be outed."

"People don't always think of the consequences of their actions."

"When did you become so philosophical?" Gavin asked.

"I've been hanging around you." I smiled.

The server brought over our coffee, but she didn't look any calmer. "Have you decided on what you want?"

"A Netwood hamburger." I wasn't in the mood to think too much, and this was their specialty—or so the menu claimed.

"The same," Gavin said.

After we told her how well we liked them done, and what kind of sides we wanted, the server left. "If we could get into the morgue, we could see if the sheriff has those marks in his neck, not that vampires can't kill in a lot of different ways if death is their goal."

"Sneaking into the morgue isn't going to happen," Gavin said.

"I wasn't thinking that *we'd* go." I wiggled my eyebrows.

"Ah, got it. If Bella was able to magically enter the morgue on that cruise you two were on, she can go into this morgue."

"Exactly."

He sipped on his coffee. "Suppose she finds out that your hypothesis is correct. Then what?"

Then what indeed? "I don't know, but more and more, I'm convinced that vampires are somehow connected to Lara's death. How, precisely, I don't know. Nor am I saying one of them ran her off the road, though they could have."

"Don't discount the idea that the killer could have been a vampire slayer instead of a vampire."

"If that is the case, why would a vampire slayer want to keep Lara quiet about vampires?"

Gavin's eyes widened. "Can we say chaos? You know that the general population isn't ready to learn about ghosts, let alone vampires. People would leave this town in droves."

"That's a scary thought. How about we have this discussion with Lorenzo? I've made a lot of erroneous assumptions about his kind already. At least he can set us straight before we get too far afield."

Gavin smiled. "I like a cautious woman."

Our meal arrived less than ten minutes later, and as soon as I dug in, I groaned. I hadn't realized how hungry I was. Crime solving must use a lot of energy.

Before we settled the bill, I asked the waitress if we could buy a piece of lettuce for my pet iguana. Iggy hated being referred to as a pet, but I wasn't about to explain that he'd been teleported to town to help solve a crime, or that he was a talking iguana. Nope. This town—or most towns—weren't ready to hear that either.

"Sure. No problem." The frazzled waitress left and returned with a small box. "It's on the house."

I smiled. "Thank you."

Naturally, we left her a good tip. The moment we stepped out of the warm, cozy diner, the cold wind blasted me in the face, and I shivered in part because the sun had hidden behind the clouds. Bummer. "Brrr."

Gavin wrapped an arm around my shoulders. "I hope that when I become a resident, I'm not stationed in a cold climate." He ducked his face against the chilly breeze.

"You and me both."

Even though it was a relatively short walk to the hotel, I was happy to be inside again. When we entered our hotel room, no one was there—other than Iggy—and that worked for me. "Here is some food for you."

I opened the box and let him have his fill. "Thank you," he said in between bites.

"Iggy, did any of our friends return and then leave again?"

"No, should they have? You said you'd be gone a while."

"I know, but how long does it take to find out about an accident?" My patience had run out.

"Don't know." He dipped his head and continued eating.

I turned to Gavin. "After we speak with Cameron and snap more photos of the people in the album, maybe we can see if either the deputy or Daniel Weintraub can identify them."

"Sounds good, but who do you trust more?"

I huffed out a laugh. "That's a hard one. Neither? Both? I have no idea, other than I can't imagine Lara hooking up with someone who was a scumbag."

Gavin smiled. "I'm not sure someone's dating preference counts as proof of their honesty."

"It does to me—or rather my gut instinct says that Daniel Weintraub is a decent person."

"Did you sense some evil coming from the deputy?"

That was the problem. "No. He seemed like the type to follow the rules, so maybe he can be trusted too."

"Good to know."

Just then our trio of investigators floated in. "Phew," Lorenzo said. "That was amazing."

"What was amazing?" I asked.

"That ambulance was fast."

"Why was it moving so fast?" I thought the sheriff was dead. Or had the server been misinformed?

Bella shook her head. "The ambulance stayed under the

speed limit the whole time. Lorenzo isn't used to being in a vehicle that goes more than thirty miles an hour, that's all."

"You did learn that the sheriff is dead, right?" I asked.

"Yes. News sure travels fast," Lara said. "Anyway, we saw him, but most of him was covered in a sheet. Part of his face was exposed though, and he was white as a ghost—or is that just a saying?" She stilled. "Am I that white?"

I had thought she would have looked in a mirror by now —assuming ghosts could see their image. "Not white, exactly. Translucent is a better word." I lifted a hand. "Back to the sheriff. I'm guessing his lack of color could mean someone sucked out his blood, right?"

Lorenzo moved in front of everyone. "How did you know?"

"Lucky guess?"

"You are right. I didn't see his neck, but considering his color, a vampire was involved. I figured either that was a very thirsty one or the vampire meant to kill the sheriff."

I looked over at Gavin. "It might have been meant as a message to the community to keep away from your kind."

My boyfriend nodded. "If that's the case, then we need to heed the warning too."

A cold chill raced up my body, and it wasn't from any ghost passing through me.

"Have Hugo watch over you two," Iggy suggested.

"He's watching over Cameron." We'd asked Hugo here for that very purpose.

"This Cameron guy will be okay if he doesn't have the album, right?" Iggy finished off his lettuce. From his tone, he couldn't believe I hadn't thought of that.

At times, Iggy really surprised me. "You might be right." I turned to Lara. "Do you think your brother would be willing to let us keep the photo album in the hotel safe, especially if it meant it could help save his life?"

I was stretching the truth a bit, or so I hoped.

"If you tell him what happened to the sheriff, I bet he will. Cameron was never a risk taker. It's why he went into podiatry."

I didn't see how one related to the other, but I didn't say anything. My cell phone said it was almost two o'clock. "Did you three see the deputy anywhere?"

"Yes, he was in charge of investigating the sheriff's death," Bella said.

"Then he must have realized that a vampire was involved," I said.

Lorenzo shook his head. "Not necessarily. Even when I knew the vampire who'd bitten the person, the cops were in denial about us. Trust me, that made our life easier."

That wasn't very encouraging.

"How about if a couple of us head on over to the sheriff's office and see what's going on? The deputy might be talking to the mayor or a city councilmember about it," Lara said.

She was on top of things. "Excellent idea."

"Can I go?" Iggy asked.

"Are you willing to crawl to the sheriff's office? It's pretty far for you."

"They can't carry me?"

Iggy seemed to have forgotten that ghosts didn't have a form. "No. They aren't special like Hugo."

"Oh. Never mind then."

I nodded to Lara, and the group disappeared. "I have to say it is handy to have invisible beings around who are able to listen in on conversations and report back," I said. "But not being able to open drawers and such is kind of an issue."

"Very true," Gavin said.

Iggy finished his lettuce meal. "What's next?"

"When we go over to Lara's brother's house to deal with

the album, maybe you can tell Hugo—without Cameron hearing you—that we need Hugo to return with us."

Iggy cocked his head. "What am I supposed to do? Hold up a sign?"

Smart aleck. "I don't know. You can't communicate with him another way?"

"Where have you been? I talk to him, but I receive what he says telepathically."

"Fine, maybe when we leave, I'll motion for you to come. Instead, of calling your name, I'll call you Hugo."

The iguana stared at me. "And that helps how?"

"Maybe Hugo will say something to you, and you can nod, indicating he should return with us."

"He won't know what a nod means."

"Okay, so my plan needs some work."

While we waited for our snoops to return, I thought I'd catch Glinda up on what was going on. Plus, I figured she'd want to see that Iggy was okay.

"I'm going to do a video chat with Glinda. You up for talking to her?"

"What would you do if I said no?"

What had gotten into him? "After we solve the case, you can stay here."

"No, no. I was only kidding. I thought I could bribe you out of another few weeks of flower deliveries."

Teenagers. They were too clever. I called my cousin, and Glinda answered right away. "Hey. Is everything okay?"

I smiled. "Yes. Hugo is keeping watch over Lara's brother, and Iggy is nice and warm."

He crawled over. "I'm good."

"I miss you." Glinda blew kisses at him.

Iggy looked up at me. "Tell her not to do that gooey stuff. It embarrasses me."

I laughed. "She can hear you, you know. You aren't invisible or silent."

"I know. That's why I'm working with Hugo to see if I can be like him."

Oh, boy.

"Iggy," Glinda said, "have you solved the case yet?"

"No. I just arrived."

"Then you better get cracking."

I smiled. I loved the way she dealt with him. "I need to tell you our good news," I said.

"I so love good news," she said.

"Gavin can now hear Iggy! The spell that Levy's coven performed extended to familiars. Is that not cool or what?"

"That is wonderful. It certainly made my life easier when Jaxson could communicate with him."

"Speaking of Jaxson, did he ever find out anything about the people in the photos?"

She shook her head. "No, and it's driving him crazy. It's like they disappeared from the face of the Earth."

"That's odd."

Glinda nodded. "We're thinking they might have been put into a kind of witness protection program. I know they aren't witnesses to a crime, but they could still be in danger of being bitten again."

"True, but if nobody believe in vampires, they wouldn't support moving a lot of people to a safe location," I said. "Not only that, I doubt Netwood would contact the Justice Department. There would be too many questions—mostly about the sanity of the sheriff's department."

"That's true, but if they *did* believe in vampires, I bet they'd move them to prevent them from spilling the beans about vampires. You know how hard our werewolves work to keep their existence secret."

"Okay, but I can't imagine someone building a compound

for them." I shivered at that thought. "Unless, it's the vampires themselves who made these people disappear."

"Let's hope not. That takes evil to a new level," Glinda said.

For the next half hour, we moved away from that depressing thought and focused more on who might have harmed Lara. "What do you think?" I asked after we'd tossed around a lot of different scenarios.

"It does seem as if Lara's finding that album triggered fear in someone."

"I agree. I just wish I knew whether a vampire slayer or a vampire wanted her dead."

"You better hope it's not the vampire," she said.

That could be painful or deadly. "Very true."

chapter fourteen

ONCE GLINDA, Gavin, and I—and Iggy— exhausted our options for what might have happened to Lara, we disconnected. As if they were waiting for me to finish my call, our ghostly beings blew in.

I could use some good news—or any news. "Well?"

"The deputy is quite frantic over the sheriff's death. Maybe that's why he let the vampire go."

Bella flew to the end of the bed—her favorite spot. "It was so frustrating. I really wanted to talk to the guy, but he couldn't see me or hear me. I thought that being a vampire would have given him some magical abilities."

"Whoa. Back up a minute. Did the deputy say why he released the man?" I asked.

"He spoke to someone about it, but I don't know who he called. I think he said he didn't have any evidence to hold him," Bella said.

"Rihanna, the deputy probably called a lawyer," Gavin said.

"Most likely. Now that the sheriff is dead, whatever he knew about this guy might never surface." Dead ends were so irritating.

"Do you think that's why the sheriff was killed?" Lorenzo asked.

"Maybe. Are vampires vengeful?" Humans were, so why not his kind.

"Some are. Some aren't."

That didn't help much.

"Lara," Gavin said. "Did the deputy mention the word *vampire* in his conversation to this person?"

"No."

Gavin glanced over at me. "I wonder if the sheriff kept the deputy and others in the dark about their existence."

"I don't know, but whoever looks at the sheriff's body will see puncture wounds—assuming a vampire sucked out some of his blood."

"Like I said, the deputy, or whoever views the sheriff, might not think a vampire did it, but rather some kind of fork-like weapon punctured his neck. That's what happened in New Orleans all the time," Lorenzo added. "As for the lack of blood, I don't know."

"I see."

It made sense that the medical examiner or the deputy wouldn't consider vampires as the cause of death if they were unaware that they existed. To be honest, if I hadn't seen the stake in Lorenzo's ghostly body, I wouldn't have either. I turned to him. "If the man was a vampire, why couldn't he see Bella? I thought you all had quite a lot of magic."

"Some of us have more than others," he said.

"Have you ever seen a ghost? When you were alive, I mean?"

"No."

That didn't help. "I'm a little rusty on my vampire lore. Do vampires—or rather your kind of vampire—do spells?"

"No. Only witches and warlocks do spells. I know for a fact that when a vampire dies, a witch does an incantation to make sure that the body stays preserved. When—or rather if—my stake is removed, in theory, I will once again be a young, healthy, and very handsome man."

Confident much? "Sounds great. I guess since you are a ghost, whatever magical powers you might have had are gone, right? Other than being able to change into an animal, that is."

"We tested that theory when I first met you two," Lorenzo said. "Truth is, I never cared all that much about what talents I had—other than being able to hypnotize someone so they would do what I wanted. I had everything I needed."

Everything but teeth that would grow when he wanted to suck someone's blood. For the people's sake in New Orleans, that was a good thing.

"Aren't we going to tell Rihanna and Gavin about the sheriff's wife?" Bella asked.

"What? You saw the sheriff's wife? Where?" These three were not great at delivering information.

"I'll tell them," Bella said as she faced us. "When we arrived at the station, Mrs. Schlemmer was beside herself, as you would expect. She was crying and yelling at the same time."

"Yelling at the deputy?" I asked.

"Yes. Something about everything her husband worked for would be for nothing if the deputy didn't keep how her husband died under wraps."

Wow. "Wait a minute, the sheriff's wife doesn't want anyone to know how he died?"

"I assume that's what *keep it under wraps* means," Bella said.

I looked over at Gavin. "That implies she knows a vampire killed him."

"Rihanna, you can't jump to that conclusion, though it's what I think happened."

"We need confirmation on *how* he died." I turned to Bella. "Remember when you went into the morgue on the boat?"

"Yes. Say no more. Lorenzo and I can check out the morgue here. We'll find out if there are puncture wounds in the sheriff's neck. If we could handle a camera, we would take pictures."

"Too bad Hugo isn't here right now. He could help," Iggy said.

"True," I said.

"Do you know where the morgue is located?" Bella asked.

Gavin jumped up and opened his computer. It took a half minute to find the cross streets. "Come over here, and I can show you on the map."

All three floated over to his computer. After studying it for a few seconds, Bella nodded. "We shouldn't be gone long, unless we decide to see what the autopsy person says."

"The doctor won't start cutting him open right away," Gavin said. "It takes some preparation."

Bella shrugged. "Whatever."

It was actually good to hear that word come out of Bella's mouth. It kind of defined who she was.

Lara spun around to face me. "While I'm thinking of it, did you call my brother to see if we can see him after work today?"

"Not yet, but I can leave a message on his phone to see if it's okay."

Lara nodded. "Do that. He checks his messages often."

"That's good to know."

"Come on, guys," Bella said. "We'll find out what Cameron says when we return. Time to do a little investigating."

I did love her attitude. I texted Cameron and said we'd like to come over after work since we had more information on Lara's case. I figured that would interest him. Less than ten minutes later, Cameron responded that he'd be home by quarter after five.

"We're all set," I told Gavin.

"I'm going with you, remember?" Iggy said.

"Absolutely." I turned back to Gavin. "When do you think they will start the autopsy?"

"That depends on how busy the medical examiner is. Given the size of Netwood, the doctor might start prepping the body right away. Finding out who killed the sheriff will be of utmost importance to the town."

"I bet you're right. It would be easy for our ghosts to check out the condition of the sheriff if he is already on the table when they arrive."

"Agreed."

"In the meantime, we should go over to the medical center with the pictures of the people with the neck wounds. Lara thought they might have been photographed there."

"It's as good a time as ever," he said.

I turned to Iggy. "When our friends return, can you tell them that Gavin and I are going to investigate the people from the photo album."

"Didn't you tell Lara that she could come with you?" Iggy reminded me.

Darn. "Yes, but that was before we learned the sheriff was dead."

"Fine."

Gavin wrapped an arm around my waist. "Come on, time is of the essence."

Iggy cleared his throat, or rather he made some iguana noise that was meant to grab our attention. I spun around. "How long will you be gone?" he asked.

"However much time it takes," Gavin answered, "but I don't expect it to be too long."

"Okay. I'll stay here then."

Not that we'd asked him to come with us this time. I stepped over to Iggy and picked him up. "Would you like me to find the remote so you can watch television?" I doubted he knew how to use the hotel remote or was able to use it. These buttons were small.

"No, that's okay. I'll stare out the window and dream of sand, beaches, and sunshine."

I chuckled. "You do that, buddy."

Gavin had already noted the directions to the clinic, so we took off. Once we had slipped into the car, he turned the key, firing up the engine. He glanced over at me. "I hope you haven't gotten your hopes up about the clinic telling us a lot?"

I always tried to stay grounded. "I know they aren't going to admit that the two people who came in were bitten by a vampire."

Gavin nodded and pulled out into the flow of traffic. "What do you hope to learn then?"

"What date they came in and what the patient said happened. If Lorenzo is right, and vampires hypnotize their victims, the person might not know much."

"That's a reasonable expectation."

We found the clinic with no trouble. Unfortunately, the young receptionist was no help at all, other than she told us that both victims seemed to have been in one of their examination rooms when their photo was taken.

"Could you look up when Caitlyn Shorter and Kathy Dumont were in here."

"I'm afraid I can't. If you want the information, you'll need a patient release form signed."

That was the problem. We needed to find them first. And if we did, we could ask them directly. We thanked her and left.

"That was a bust," I said.

"Yes, but we learned the victims—if that is what they were

—sought help, which means they might have told others what happened."

"That's great if we can find out who they talked with. When we look at the photo album again, maybe we'll learn whether any of the others are still in town, and then we can talk to them."

"Fingers crossed," he said.

When we returned to the hotel, our three guests were there. "Hey, how did it go?" I asked.

"Lorenzo is a wuss," Bella said.

"Why is that?"

"I'll tell it," he said. "That doctor had cut open the sheriff, and when I saw his insides, I almost felt sick."

I didn't think ghosts could have an upset stomach. Clearly, my knowledge of them was lacking. Glinda would be so interested to learn more about them too. "I'm sorry, but what about the cause of death?"

"A bite to the neck," Bella said.

"Did the doctor say anything about it being from a vampire?" Gavin asked.

"Not on the recorder," Lara answered. "When the assistant asked what caused the two punctures, the doctor said he'd have to take tissue samples, but I had the sense he knew."

Gut instincts wouldn't cut it in court. Of course, testimony by a ghost wouldn't happen either. "When the doctor sends the report to the deputy—who I guess will be the sheriff, at least temporarily— maybe we can get a glimpse of it."

"If my mom did the autopsy, you know she'd never mention magic in a report. She'd say it appeared to be a puncture wound, but that she hadn't identified the exact object that would have caused it."

"Darn," I said. "Someone has to know."

"Another vampire slayer might have heard about the cause of death," Lorenzo said.

"Do you know any of them?" I asked. "I bet they don't go around town wearing a T-shirt that says they are one."

"No," he said.

"Rihanna, if vampire slayers were open about the existence of vampires, no one would have tried to run Lara off the road," Gavin said.

"That's assuming her death had to do with her letting the cat out of the bag, so to speak," I shot back.

Iggy crawled over to me. "You don't have squat, do you?"

"Way to rub it in, buddy."

"Just saying. Maybe you should use Hugo to find out a few things."

That wasn't a bad idea. Hugo had the ability to make people confess things. While it couldn't be used in court—unless it was under special circumstances—it would help us know where to focus our efforts. "That is a brilliant idea, Detective Iggy."

"All in a day's work." He turned around, dropped onto his stomach and closed his eyes.

Really?

chapter fifteen

"DO you have news about who ran my sister off the road?" Cameron Hackett asked as he motioned us inside his home.

Iggy was snuggled inside of Gavin's coat, in part because he didn't like the cold, and partly because I wasn't in the mood to explain to Cameron why I had an iguana with us. If he had been able to communicate with Iggy, I would have shown him.

"We have a theory, but it will seem strange to you."

"Stranger than the fact my sister is a ghost?" He looked around. "Is she here by the way?"

"Yes."

Gavin and I sat on the sofa while Cameron asked if we wanted something to drink. Since our conversation might take a while, we told him coffee would be great.

As soon as he disappeared, I saw my chance to contact Hugo. "Hugo, where are you?" I whispered.

Iggy poked his head out of Gavin's jacket. "He's here," Iggy said. "You can talk to him."

"Hugo, if Cameron gives us the album, we need you to come back to the hotel with us. Okay?"

Iggy nodded and faced us. "He'll do that. He said

watching the doctor check out feet all day wasn't his favorite thing to do anyway."

I cracked a smile. "I totally understand."

Not long after my discussion with Hugo, Cameron carried in a tray of drinks and placed it on the table. Next to the coffee were both cream and sugar. "Thanks."

He sat down. "What is your theory?"

"First, did you hear the sheriff was murdered?"

"Yes. That was so sad. Do you know what happened to him?"

I explained that Lara and two of her ghost friends went into the morgue and saw the puncture wounds in the sheriff's neck. "While we can't be positive, it seems as if he was killed by a vampire."

I gave him more details about what Lorenzo said.

Cameron blew out a breath. "So, we're back to vampires again?"

"It seems so." I explained that we were thinking that either a vampire or a vampire slayer ran Lara off the road, though I had no evidence either way.

"Why would you point a finger at vampires? Because she found out about them?" Cameron asked.

"Yes. It's why we think it would be wise if you don't hold onto the album. We don't want you to be next on the hit list."

Cameron dipped his chin. "What do you suggest I do with it?"

"Let us put it in the hotel safe."

He vehemently shook his head. "I am not putting you two in jeopardy."

I figured he'd say that. As much as I hadn't wanted to scare him to death, it was time he found out about Hugo. "We'll have protection."

"The deputy is too busy to be your bodyguard."

Naturally, he'd assumed we meant we'd hire a human.

"If ghosts and vampires aren't enough to wrap your head around, be prepared to have your mind blown even more." I looked around the room." Hugo, would you show yourself?"

Hugo appeared behind Cameron. "Who is Hugo?" he asked.

"If I told you, you wouldn't believe me." I nodded behind him.

Cameron whipped around. "Where did you come from?" His voice cracked.

"It's a long story," I said. "For starters, Hugo can make himself invisible. In fact, he's been protecting you all day in case someone tried to harm you."

"I think you're imagination has gotten the best of you, young lady."

Hugo demonstrated his ability to disappear. When he reappeared, Cameron's hand shot to his chest. "You weren't kidding."

"No."

"Iggy, you can come out too," I said.

"And who is that?" Cameron asked.

It would take us hours to give him the full rundown. Furthermore, I doubt he'd believe most of it. "Iggy is my cousin's...pet. But he can communicate with Hugo, since Hugo is mute."

"Dare I ask *what* Hugo is? Don't tell me he's a vampire too."

I blew out a breath. "No, he's a gargoyle shifter who can teleport and cloak himself. With a touch of a hand, he can temporarily paralyze a person. No vampire could get within ten feet of us if Hugo is around."

"What exactly is he doing in my house?"

I'd just explained that, but I understood how overwhelming this was to Cameron. "Like I said, he's been protecting you in case anyone wanted to harm you because you have the album."

Cameron took off his glasses and rubbed his eyes. "I'm a scientist. None of this is making any sense. Vampires, ghosts, and now disappearing men? What else is there?"

"A lot more, but right now, we need you to be very careful."

He held up a hand. "I will, but please let me know when my life can return to normal." Cameron stood. "I'll get the album for you. I want nothing more to do with it."

That was easier than I thought. "Thanks. And if anyone asks you about it, feel free to tell them that we have the photos. I'd love to catch either a vampire slayer or a vampire."

"Not a problem."

Cameron disappeared down the hall, and Gavin clasped my hand. "He'll be okay. Eventually."

"I'm not so sure. Seeing a person appear out of thin air can cause you to doubt your sanity."

"It did for me at first, but now I just accept it." He leaned over and kissed me.

"Get a room," Bella said, and I laughed.

Cameron came back with the album. "When this is over, what will you do with this?"

That was an excellent question. "Since there will always be vampires and those who hunt them, maybe it should be destroyed."

"Maybe, but let's discuss it before you do."

"Sure."

Iggy suddenly disappeared, and I assumed Hugo had cloaked himself again and then picked up Iggy. It was for the best that he travel with Hugo back to the hotel to minimize his exposure to the cold.

After we thanked Cameron and assured him we would do

what we could to find out the truth about his sister, Gavin and I left.

When we slipped into the car, Hugo appeared in the back seat with Iggy. So much for returning to the hotel. Interesting. Hopefully, he hadn't sat on any of the three ghosts, not that they'd mind.

"Hugo says he's sorry," Iggy said.

"Sorry for what?" I asked as I turned around. Gavin started the car and pulled out of the driveway.

"For startling Cameron."

"I asked Hugo to appear." Since when had Hugo become sensitive?

Iggy snuggled closer to Hugo. Considering he could transform into a granite statue, I was surprised he could provide much warmth for an iguana.

"Hugo, if you want to take Iggy back to the hotel room, that would be okay."

He nodded and disappeared.

"Phew," Bella said. "I hadn't realized how big that man is."

Hugo immediately returned to the car. "What's wrong?" I asked.

Now that he didn't have Iggy with him, communicating with him would be impossible. He pointed to the album.

"I think he is saying you might be in danger now that you have the album," Bella said. "He wants to protect you."

She figured that out from a finger point? Maybe she did. "Thank you." I handed him the album. "How about you flip through the pages for Lara to see if she knows any of these people?"

He nodded. Lara asked him to slow down a few times. "I know several of these people—or rather I did. I don't recall seeing them of late."

"There is no way all fifty of these people moved out of

town." Unless these victims were being held in a kind of prison. Even to me, that sounded crazy.

When we returned to the hotel, Lara repeated all of the names she could remember, and I jotted them down. Unfortunately, she wasn't friends with any of them, so she didn't have their phone numbers.

"How about we ask Daniel to help?" Lara suggested. "He's connected."

"That's a good idea. It's past office hours though, so maybe tomorrow we can stop by his office."

"I could call and see if he was willing to come over—" Lara stopped. "Sorry, I forgot he can't hear me."

That would be tough. "I could call him."

"That would be great." She probably just wanted to see Daniel again, and I couldn't blame her.

Lorenzo tapped the stake protruding from his heart, but of course, his hand went right through it. "I have an idea. How about if I try to find the man who the sheriff brought in and ask him what happened to all of these people?"

"You mean the vampire?" I asked.

"Yes. I might be able to extract some information out of him."

Lorenzo, too, seemed to have forgotten that he was dead. "How can you do that? If you ask him questions, he can't see or hear you. When you were on the boat, Genevieve had been there to record the confession."

"I don't need to talk in order to extract information. Remember, I can hypnotize people."

"I remember all too well."

"How about if Lorenzo, Hugo, and I find this guy?" Iggy asked."

I looked over at Gavin. "What do you think?"

"Nothing will happen to Iggy if that is what you're worried about."

"Okay, but don't stay out too long, you three."

Hugo nodded, and they disappeared.

"I still think Daniel can help," Lara said.

"I plan to give him a call." Once she told me his personal cell, I dialed his number.

"Daniel Weintraub."

"Hi, this is Rihanna Samuels, the friend of Lara's ghost?" I felt a little silly saying that.

"Trust me, I remember."

"Did you ever learn the name of the woman we asked you about?"

"Yes, her name is Brenda Wilson."

I waited for him to tell me where she lived, but he said nothing further. "Is she in town?"

"Actually, no. I tried to find out more about her whereabouts, but it's as if she disappeared from the face of the Earth. Good thing we aren't talking about aliens. That would really freak me out."

Me, too. "That's what my sister's fiancé said. All the people we were able to track down seemed to have walked into a void."

"What can I do?" he asked.

I explained that I had the photo album of the vampire victims. "There have to be fifty people in there, all with marks on their necks. I know it's late, but would you be willing to stop by our hotel room and see if you can identify any of them. Lara already told us what she knows."

"How did she do that?"

How quickly people forget. "She might be dead, but she had no problem communicating."

Daniel let out a big breath. "What I wouldn't give to be able to see and talk to her again."

"I understand, but you can't touch a ghost."

"I get it. Where are you staying?"

I gave him the name of the hotel and our room number. "We'll be waiting."

As soon as I disconnected, I turned to Gavin. "I hope we are doing the right thing in trusting Daniel."

Lara flew in front of us. "I trust him."

"Okay."

Sure enough, Daniel arrived in under ten minutes. When he stepped into our room, he looked around. "Lara, are you here?"

She immediately flew to him and wrapped her ghostly self around him. "Tell him that I am here."

I smiled. "I think he knows. I saw him shiver."

"Oh, I keep forgetting." She moved away.

Daniel Weintraub cleared his throat. "Where would you like to set up?"

I wasn't sure there was more to it than flipping through a few pages of a book, but I nodded to the small table in the room. I opened my laptop, ready to take notes. For the next five minutes, he listed about fifteen names.

"This is great. Do you know where they live?" I asked.

"Honestly, no. I remember that Randy Franklin, who worked at the hardware store, moved away."

Ugh. "That seems to be the theme here. Is there anyone you know who is still in town?"

"I don't think so." He flipped through the pictures again. "This one is Ellen Langley. She's a friend of my sister. I can call Kim. I'm sure she will have Ellen's number."

Excitement raced through me. "That would be great."

He called her and said it was important that they contact Ellen right away. He nodded a few times and then jotted down a number. "Thanks."

"Well?" I asked once he disconnected.

chapter sixteen

"**MY SISTER SAID** that Ellen moved to Omaha a few months back. Kim has spoken with her a few times since she's left and claims that Ellen seems happy."

That didn't fit with any of our scenarios. "Could you call Ellen?"

"Why? So I can ask her about the bite marks?" Daniel asked.

"Yes. I think those marks are the key to why Lara is floating around us instead of being with us."

"I doubt she'll confess to having been bitten, but I'll ask." He dialed Ellen's number. "I'll put her on speaker if she answers."

"Great."

A woman picked up, and Daniel told her he was Kim's brother.

"Is she okay?" Ellen asked.

"Yes. She's doing great. I'm calling because of what happened to make you leave town."

She sucked in a breath. "You know about that?"

Daniel raised his brows, as surprised as I was that Ellen would be open to talk about her vampire attack. "I know that you and about fifty others had the same kind of marks on your neck. My girlfriend, Lara, was murdered a month ago, and I think it was because she knew too much. Can you help us? Please?"

I held my breath.

"I don't know what I can tell you, but how did you hear about those wounds? We were told to tell no one."

"Word travels fast around here."

"I'm sorry to hear about Lara. I hadn't heard."

"I asked Kim not to say anything."

"I understand," Ellen said.

"Who asked you to keep the attack under wraps?" he asked.

"The sheriff. He said some hate group in town was targeting random people. Apparently, they sedated me and injected me with some kind of venom. It left two big marks on my neck that took quite a while to heal."

Venom? I raised my brows at Daniel.

"What kind of venom? Snake venom?"

"I don't know. All he said was that if I remained in town, and this group injected me again, the second dose would kill me."

I wish the sheriff were alive to confirm or deny this fact. I quickly typed a question on my laptop and turned it around for Daniel to ask it.

"Have you spoken with anyone else this has happened to?" he asked.

"A few. They all said the same thing. Why?"

"I'm just trying to figure out who might have killed my girlfriend. Your information has been very useful."

"Is the sheriff close to rounding up this hate group?"

"The sheriff was murdered today."

"Oh, no!"

"Ellen, I have a feeling that it might not be safe in

Netwood for a while, but I'll have my sister call you when it's okay for you to return."

"Thank you."

Daniel disconnected. "What do you think?"

My thoughts were too jumbled to think much of anything. "A hate group? Have you heard about them?"

"No. It sounds like a coverup to me."

"She has no idea about vampires, does she?" Gavin asked.

I blew out a breath. "It doesn't seem like she has a clue. We need Lorenzo here to see if two vampire bites could kill a person."

"Definitely," Gavin said.

I turned back to Daniel. "I appreciate you calling her."

"Of course."

Just then, Hugo, Iggy, and Lorenzo returned. When Hugo and Iggy uncloaked, I thought Daniel was going to faint. "It's okay. They're with me."

"But...but...that man just appeared out of nowhere."

I went through the whole gargoyle shifter thing that I did with Cameron. "I know it's hard to believe, but Hugo here can protect us against vampires. In fact, there is another ghost with them now—Lorenzo Bambini—who has been a big help to us."

Daniel squinted and glanced around. "I wish I could see ghosts."

An idea struck. "Hugo, is it possible for you to help Daniel see Lara, Bella, and Lorenzo for a few minutes?"

Hugo looked down at Iggy who listened carefully. Iggy turned to me. "He can try. He's never done anything regarding ghosts before."

"Trying is fine." I turned to Daniel. "Hugo is going to see if maybe he can channel his abilities into you for a minute. You might be able to see and hear Lara—and the others too."

"No!" she said. "I look terrible."

"I don't think he'll care." I told him what she said.

"Lara, I know you were in an accident. I love you. I just want to talk to you and hear your voice one more time."

My heart cracked at his tender words. I nodded to Hugo. Slowly, the large man walked over to Daniel. When the lawyer stiffened, I told him he had nothing to worry about. "Most likely he'll place his hands on your temples."

Iggy nodded. "If Hugo lets go, the connection will be lost."

"Thank you, Iggy." I told Daniel what he said.

He inhaled deeply. "I'm ready."

Hugo stepped behind the man and placed his palms on the sides of Mr. Weintraub's head. Hugo's lips moved, but naturally, nothing came out. Apparently, Hugo's abilities were extensive because Daniel's eyes widened. "Lara?"

She floated in front of him. "Oh, Daniel. You can see me?"

He swallowed. "Yes," he croaked out.

"I know we only have a minute, but I'm so sorry that I didn't get the chance to tell you before I died that I would have chosen you over James." She reached out to touch him, but her arm went straight through him. "I love you."

Daniel's chin trembled for a moment. "Thank you for telling me, and I love you too!"

Hugo let go. I guess he didn't need to hear any more. Daniel Weintraub sniffled. He looked back at Hugo and then at me and Gavin. "That was the best present. Thank you for that."

"I'm glad we could help."

I turned to Lorenzo. "We spoke with one of the victims." I told them what Ellen said. "Is there any truth to the fact that a second vampire bite will kill a person?"

Lorenzo's brows pinched. "Whoever told you that is making it up."

I repeated what Lorenzo said.

"I was right," Daniel said. "They used that as an excuse to control those people."

What a shame. I faced Lorenzo. "Did you find the vampire the deputy released?"

"Yes. He couldn't see me, but Hugo was amazing."

"Did you learn anything useful about these vampire attacks?"

Lorenzo nodded. "I understand their dilemma. Vampires need blood to survive. Mind you, if humans aren't available—or if the vampires don't want to call attention to themselves—they can hunt animals and use that blood, or they can go to a blood bank."

That was consistent to what I'd seen in a few television shows. "Were they caught stealing?"

"No. Turns out the person running the blood bank is a vampire. If you didn't know, not all blood donated is useable. Some is contaminated, but we don't care."

"One man's trash is another man's treasure?" Bella chimed in.

"Exactly. But apparently, there was a shortage of blood in the blood banks for a few weeks, so the vampires had to take from the human population."

"I can guess what happened. They drew blood from about fifty people?"

He shrugged. "I didn't ask the number. According to Edgar Simmons, the vampire who was brought in, the vampires didn't want to do it, but it's who we are as a species."

We weren't here to place blame. "Did you find out what happened to all the people? Did all of them leave town?"

Lorenzo looked over at Hugo. "No."

"Tell us!" Lara said. "Sheesh. I thought I dragged out a story."

"Edgar Simmons reluctantly told us an all too familiar tale. Most of the vampires in town are upstanding individuals. We didn't press him on who was and who wasn't like me since it's not relevant. Anyway, the sheriff and many of his cohorts were determined to eliminate them."

"As in kill?" I wanted to be sure I understood.

"I believe so. These eliminators are the so-called *vampire slayers*. While Edgar didn't know the details, I pieced together that Lara's father-in-law was in charge of keeping track of who had been bitten."

"That's what the album I found was all about?" Lara asked.

"Yes," he said.

Gavin was sitting next to Daniel translating Lorenzo's tale.

"Go on," I urged. "Did he say what happened to the people?"

"He certainly didn't want to say, but between my hypnosis and Hugo's abilities, we were able to learn what he knew."

One of Hugo's main talents was making the reluctant ones talk. The beauty was that he didn't use force—just magic.

"The sheriff was able to convince many of those bitten to leave on their own. Edgar assumed that the sheriff didn't want people to panic if they learned vampires existed, and Edgar and his group didn't want to be known either."

"Was it like that for you in New Orleans?" I asked.

"Yes, but those who knew and told others were ridiculed. No one believed we really existed, which was fine by us," Lorenzo said.

"Does this vampire know where those humans who were bitten are?" Gavin asked.

"Yes. Many of them—about thirty—are being held against their will in some abandoned orphanage on the edge of town."

I waited for Gavin to translate that to Daniel. "I know where that is," Daniel said. "We need to tell...someone, but who?"

That was the problem. "The city council maybe?" I suggested. "Or the Nebraska police?"

"If what Edgar said is true, many of the local people could be vampires," Daniel stated. "Besides, I'm not sure ordinary humans have the ability to take down vampires."

That would be an issue. "We could tell Deputy Denison, but do we know for sure whether it's vampires or vampire slayers who are holding these bitten people? That would make a difference."

"I don't know," Daniel admitted.

"Why don't a few of us check out this abandoned orphanage?" Lara said. "I know where it is. Maybe Lorenzo can sense if the captors are vampires or not."

"That would be a big help. It's late though. Can you see in the dark?" I recalled Bella telling me she didn't have that ability.

"I don't know, but surely some lights will be on, and it's not like we're going to be caught," Lara said.

"That's true. Why don't you all go?" I turn to Iggy. "Except Iggy."

"Spoilsport."

Hugo shook his head, and then looked at Iggy. The adorable pink iguana lifted his head. "Hugo said he needs me in case he has to communicate with the ghosts."

I had to check with Hugo. Sometimes Iggy said things that weren't totally true. This time Hugo nodded.

"Fine, but Hugo, please hold onto him."

He dipped his chin, implying he'd never let anything happen to his good friend.

"Okay," Lara said. "Follow me, gang."

One second they were there, and the next they were gone. I turned to Daniel. "We'll find out in a few minutes if what Edgar told Lorenzo and Hugo is true or not."

Daniel stabbed his fingers through his hair. "This is unbelievable. I feel as if I am living in a dream."

"I know what you mean," Gavin said. "I've only been able to see ghosts for three days now."

"How do you deal with it?" Daniel asked.

"I trust Rihanna."

That was so sweet.

"Since I've spoken with Lara—which is a gift I will never forget—I will rely on trust too."

"Mr. Weintraub—

"Call me Daniel."

"Daniel, suppose what Edgar told the others is true—that someone is holding a lot of people hostage—and we decide to tell the deputy? Who's to say he doesn't already know about this hostage situation and actually agrees with it?"

Daniel and Gavin shared glances. "I know some law officers from another town, but it's not exactly their jurisdiction. However, before we decide what to do, let's wait for your friends to report back."

It was rather cool that he believed they could learn the truth.

What seemed like a long time later, the gang arrived. "That was really creepy," Iggy said.

I didn't like that description. "What did you find out?"

Bella floated in front. Who put her in charge, I didn't know. "For starters, the building was cloaked."

I repeated what she said to Daniel since his ability to hear and see ghosts no longer existed.

"Cloaked?" he asked.

"I'm guessing someone put a spell on the building to hide it. You've seen Hugo cloak himself." I nodded to him. One minute we could see him, and the next we couldn't. "Thank you, Hugo for the demonstration."

"When was the last time you saw this building?" Gavin asked Daniel.

He glanced to the side. "I don't know. I don't drive out there very often. Maybe six months ago."

"When do you think your sister's friend left town?" I figured there was a connection.

"About then."

I faced the group again. "If the building was cloaked, how did you know it was there?"

Lara nodded to Hugo. "He sensed it, and Iggy told us."

I relayed the information to Daniel. "What did you find inside, assuming you went in?"

"Since it was late, most of the people were in their rooms. However, a few were sitting at tables in the main room. With guards who had guns!"

"It's a jail?" I asked.

"Kind of." Bella nodded to Hugo. I'm guessing he had more to share.

Iggy and he did their communication thing, and then Iggy nodded. "Hugo said he sensed some kind of electric fence around the building."

"That's not good. Even if you could tell us exactly where the building was located, we couldn't get in."

Bella snapped her fingers then instantly frowned when she made no sound. "I have an idea."

"I love ideas.

chapter seventeen

I WAITED for Bella to tell us her big plan, but she just stood there grinning. "What is it?"

"It's time to bring in the big guns."

"Big guns?" I asked.

Gavin continued to give Daniel the blow-by-blow of what was being said.

"I'm going to ask my grandmother to help. This is right up her alley."

I immediately ran through all of the magic that Glinda, Genevieve, and the others had done, but uncloaking a building hadn't been one of them. "But your grandmother is in New Orleans."

"So? I already spoke with Hugo—through Iggy of course—and together we can teleport her here. She can call upon her friends—dead friends if you want to be exact—and they can remove all the barriers to the inside."

"Wow."

When Gavin translated, Daniel just shook his head. "Who is this grandmother?"

I answered. "I've not met her, but she is a high voodoo

priestess. I'll confess I know very little about her capabilities, but the few things that Bella shared with me in the past, I think she can do what Bella claims."

Daniel held out his palms. "I see now that I have to toss my belief systems out the window. Can I help?"

"I don't know." I looked at my phone. "Guys, it is quite late. How about tomorrow morning, Hugo, Iggy, Bella, and I guess Lorenzo and Lara, if you want, take a little road trip to New Orleans? Hopefully, Bella's grandmother is willing to help. She'll have to gather what she needs to summon the dead."

Bella smiled. "She'll come."

"Okay. Great."

When no one moved, I groaned. "Gavin and I are retiring for the night."

"Ah, got it," Bella said. "Everyone to the hallway, except Iggy, since he needs to be in a warm room."

That was sweet of her to be that considerate. Maybe belonging to a group helped her grow as a person.

Daniel stood. "I'd like to be there when this amazing event occurs."

"Sure, but let's say Bella's grandma is successful in taking down the barrier. There are men inside with guns. I don't feel comfortable knocking on the door and telling them they've committed a crime." I was being silly of course, but I was stumped.

"No, you can't. We'll need a lot of help. This might sound crazy, but can this magical person, say, freeze the guards where they stand? I've seen it done on television. And yes, I know it's all done with computer graphics."

I chuckled. "I've seen that technique too. It's a nice visual effect. Everything from the people to the objects are put into freeze frame. I doubt even a voodoo priestess can do that, but

I've been wrong before." I mentally went through some of the cases Glinda had worked on, but I didn't recall anyone stopping time like that.

"What about Hugo?" Gavin asked. "Can he do that?"

"Hugo can freeze one person—that is, paralyze him for a few seconds—but I've never heard he could incapacitate more than one at a time."

"Then we should find out how many guards they have. If this grandmother or maybe Hugo can use magic to keep them from moving for even a few minutes, those held captive could be freed. I could arrange to have a few vans or a bus take the people to safety," Daniel said.

I liked that idea. "Even if Hugo or Bella's grandmother could hold the guards at bay, the cops need to swoop in and arrest them."

"Of course."

"What about their leader?" Gavin asked.

"It would be too good to be true that he was there, though someone from the outside would need to come with food," I said.

Daniel snapped his fingers. "That's when we hit them, so to speak. Your Hugo can cloak himself. When this person shows up, he hold the person hostage until we get there."

It wasn't as if Hugo could call 911. Iggy couldn't press the buttons either, nor could anyone hear him. Bummer. "I think we'll need to be nearby, and that's not very practical."

"Rihanna, let's see what Bella tells us tomorrow and make our decision based on that," Daniel said.

That seemed to be the lawyer's go-to method of decision making. "Good idea."

Daniel slipped on his coat. "Call me tomorrow morning, and I'll come right over. I want to see this to the end."

"Thank you."

Once he left, I dropped onto the bed. "Do you think we'll really find these people and figure out who killed Lara?"

Gavin sat next to me. "You are Rihanna Samuels, mind reader and person extraordinaire. I believe in you."

My heart soared. "I wish I did."

I had just washed up the next morning when the gang arrived. Hugo opened the door and led in Cassandra Maurel, a tiny woman in her mid-sixties wearing a white turban and a colorful muumuu. Her wrists were adorned with multi-colored bracelets, and her necklace appeared to be made of bones. All in all, she was kind of a scary looking woman, but I painted on my happy face, nonetheless.

I held out my hand. "I'm Rihanna. Thank you so much, Ms. Maurel, for coming."

"I could never say no to Bella. She can be very persuasive."

I chuckled. "Tell me about it."

"Sit down, Grandma," Bella said as she motioned her grandmother take a seat at the table.

No sooner had she taken off her coat than a knock sounded on the door. "That should be our lawyer friend who is helping with the case."

"I told her all about Daniel," Lara said.

"Good." That would save time.

Gavin opened the door, led him in, and introduced Daniel to the voodoo priestess.

He smiled. "It's nice to see a human for a change."

She chuckled, looking a lot less threatening. "I understand."

There were four chairs, so Gavin, Daniel, and I joined

Bella's grandmother. "Did Bella explain the situation?" I asked her.

"She did."

"Do you think you can help us?" I figured she could or she wouldn't have traveled here.

"I believe I can. I have the items I need to call upon my ancestors to help. Normally, I wouldn't bother them, but Bella and her friends told me about all of those affected. We certainly can't have some vampire haters do that to those innocent people."

I slowly let out the breath I was holding. "No. That's kidnapping, not to mention a few other charges." I didn't know what those would be, but it didn't matter. "What do you need from us?"

"Hugo, with Iggy's help, told me he can cloak me and teleport me into the building to see what I'm dealing with. I need to understand how much space I have."

That gave me an idea. "That sounds good. How about if after Hugo shows you what is going on—with our ghosts, of course— he returns and takes me to see the site. I have an idea."

"Rihanna?" Gavin sounded worried.

"It will be fine. I want to take a video of what is going on inside. I figure it will make it easier for Daniel to convince his police friends to help. No one will see me since Hugo will hold me and keep me cloaked." I turned to him. "You can do that, right?"

The small smile and then the nod implied it would be a piece of cake. Once Hugo placed Iggy on his shoulder, he swept Bella's grandmother in his arms, and it looked as if he was lifting a small sack of potatoes. And then they disappeared.

Gavin turned to me. "I like the idea of the video, but if you are invisible, how can you see the camera to use it?"

I'd thought of that. "I'll use the camera on my phone. It's simpler than my SLR. I'll set it to video before I leave. I just need to tap and swipe, and I'll be good to go—or so I hope. Just in case, I'll practice with Hugo beforehand."

"Are you going to take Iggy with you so you can communicate with Hugo?" Gavin asked.

"No. If I talk, or if Iggy speaks and there are any witches around, people will hear us. I don't intend to do anything other than take a short video." I faced Daniel. "I trust a video showing people milling about with men holding guns on them would be sufficient for the law to investigate?"

"I should hope so."

Gavin tapped the table. "We forgot to ask Bella's grandmother if she can freeze time—if that is the right term for it."

I nodded. "We'll ask when she returns."

"Great. One more thing. I don't think we should mention to anyone that Bella's grandmother plans to summon the dead in order to remove the cloaking, or that she can somehow deactivate the electric fence," Gavin said. "That would totally spook the lawmen."

Daniel nodded. "Amen to that."

We didn't have to wait long before the group popped back into view. Gavin pulled out the fourth chair at the table. "Put her down here, Hugo."

Hugo placed Cassandra gently on the seat and stepped back.

"How did it go, and what did you find?" I was very anxious to know if Edgar told the truth.

She blew out a breath. "It was quite sad. Hugo teleported me to the center of the activity. I only spotted a few people sitting on sofas reading or at tables talking quietly in the main room. Two guards with large guns were standing watch."

I had so many questions, I didn't know where to begin. "Was the place invisible?"

"I don't know. We went straight to the inside."

"Yes," Bella said. "Lorenzo and I checked the outside once I knew my grandmother was okay. You couldn't see a thing, other than some big empty lot."

"I trust you didn't test the existence of the electric fence Edgar claims is there?"

"No," Bella said. "That would be outside of our ghostly abilities."

"I could have tested it," Iggy said, "but I had to stay with Hugo."

Good thing he didn't or he might have been electrocuted. Sheesh. "No one talked, did they?"

"No, though even if they heard us, what could they do? We were invisible." Iggy sounded quite excited to be on the adventure.

Gavin turned to Cassandra. "Is there a way to immobilize the guards long enough for the police to free the people?"

She pressed her lips together and then nodded. "That can be arranged."

I wanted to ask her how she planned to do that, but I figured that would be like asking a magician to reveal his secrets.

"Great." I looked over at Gavin. "When Hugo takes me there, how do you suppose we test the fence?" I asked.

"Don't worry about that," Cassandra said. "When I take away the spell for the invisibility shield, I'll make sure the electric fence doesn't work."

I wondered if she planned to unplug it or do a spell to shut down the entire power grid? I honestly hadn't interacted with a voodoo priestess before and didn't want to sound disrespectful.

"Tell us more about what you found inside," Daniel said.

"Like Bella told you, I, too, saw several people in the main room. Hugo seemed to know where to go, because next thing I knew, he'd whisked me into a few bedrooms where the people were either reading or watching television. I didn't see any computers. I guess they wanted these people to remain isolated. I will say the place was clean and looked fairly nice."

"Maybe it keeps the people from rebelling," I said.

"Perhaps. I'm sure they've been told that an attempt to escape could prove fatal."

That was very unsettling.

"I wonder who delivers the food, medical care, and other needs?" Daniel asked. "If we could learn who runs the facility, it would help. I'm guessing those with the guns are merely hired hands."

"Or they are vampire slayer fanatics," I said.

"Or that."

I pushed back my chair and approached Hugo. With my phone in hand, I was ready to take a video of the room. "Hugo, can you cloak both of us for a minute? I want to see if I can use my camera while I'm unable to see it."

"Hugo wants to know if you mean now?" Iggy asked.

"Yes."

Hugo placed a hand on my shoulder, and I disappeared, as did the phone in my hand. Since I could feel it, I pressed the button where I thought it was and held the phone out. I had no idea what I was videotaping, but I figured if I moved it around slowly, I'd record something important. After about thirty seconds, I told Hugo I was finished, and I appeared.

I stopped the video and replayed it. "Not bad. I held it out at shoulder height, so I managed to capture most of you in the picture."

Satisfied I could do this, I set the camera up again and then turned to Hugo. "I need you to teleport me to the main room and then maybe to a few other rooms. I will be videotaping the whole time. When I tap your hand three times, that means we need to return here. Any questions?"

I swear he rolled his eyes as he shook his head. I held out my camera and nodded. A second later I was inside of the building, and what I saw sickened me too.

chapter eighteen

FROM CASSANDRA'S DESCRIPTION, this abandoned orphanage now resembled an old folks' home. What she failed to tell me was that a few children were there too. Had they been bitten? Or had the people in charge decided there would be less fuss if those attacked had their whole family with them?

I was so consumed with what I was seeing that I almost forgot to press the record button. Hoping it was running, I rotated my arms around in a semi-circle. I really wanted to take an up close photo of some of these people to match them to those in the album. Since there was quite a lot of chatter, I leaned my head back and whispered to Hugo. "Can we move in close to the people?"

Naturally, Hugo didn't answer, but he did zoom us in to a few of the captives. Once more, I had no idea if what I was filming caught their faces or if I was photographing the ceiling. I could only hope my experience with a camera helped guide me. I figured we could return to take more pictures of the rooms if need be. I tapped his hand three times, and before I could take a breath, we were back in the hotel room.

When he set me down, I became visible again. "Being invisible is not all it's cracked up to be," I said. "I couldn't tell if I captured anything." I turned around to Hugo. "Thank you."

He nodded. I went over to the table, hoping I had some good footage. I placed the phone on the table for all to see. Naturally, our ghosts hovered over us while Iggy crawled up Hugo's leg. He must have told Hugo that he wanted to watch, because Hugo came over too.

I'd taken about a two minute video. The part that included the main room was quite good, but I missed my mark at first when I tried to zoom in on a few faces.

"Stop there," Lara said.

"What did you see?"

"That's Caitlyn Shorter," Lara said.

"I thought you said she moved away from Netwood?"

"I thought that too."

"What does that mean?" Cassandra asked.

Gavin pulled out his phone and showed Bella's grandmother the photo of Caitlyn. "She is one of the women who we believe was bitten by a vampire."

The grandmother leaned forward. "Oh, yes. That is a vampire mark. I've seen many."

I loved the additional confirmation. "I guess what Edgar, the vampire, told Hugo—or rather what information Hugo and Lorenzo extracted from Edgar—was accurate. So now what?"

"Can you send me that video?" Daniel asked. "I'll need to show it to my law enforcement friends.

"Sure." Since we both had the same type of phone, it was easy to transfer the video from mine to his. "How are we going to coordinate the law enforcement with Cassandra and her fellow..." I didn't know what they were called.

"Dead ancestors is good enough." She smiled.

"Dead ancestors. Got it. If you and your *family* can

uncloak the building, how long will the spell last? Minutes, hours, or is it permanent?"

"It will be long enough. Here is my plan."

We all leaned forward and hung on her every word. When she was done, I had to sort through the series of events that Cassandra had planned and then figure out where we fit in.

"You know Gavin, Daniel, and I would like to be there—alongside the lawmen—but it is crucial that we remain hidden until Cassandra and her group remove the cloaking from the building. Timing is everything."

"Food is the key," Iggy said.

"You're hungry? Can it wait?"

He told Hugo to place him on the table. Clearly, Iggy wanted to be center stage. The only person who couldn't hear him was Daniel, so Gavin once more gave him a quick summary of what Iggy said.

"Like you said. The people need to eat, so we wait until the delivery truck arrives. The truck driver would know that the building was cloaked, right? How else could he find the place?"

Iggy was quite insightful. "Yes, but how would the truck get inside if the driver can't see anything."

Iggy turned to Cassandra. "Can a person wear special glasses or something to see the building?"

She smiled. "No, my little pink friend. At least not that I'm aware of, but the person could do a quick spell to guide the vehicle inside. Or, if there is a driveway that we didn't notice, the driver could press a button to raise the garage door and drive in."

"That's genius," I said. "Hugo, could you check it out? But before you go, how about taking a picture in case there is a driveway? The more information we have the better."

I handed him my phone, but he shook his head. He then

withdrew his phone and waved it. I'm guessing he used it for texting Genevieve since he couldn't talk on it.

"Hugo said he can do that," Iggy told us.

Hugo disappeared, and then returned sixty seconds later. He handed me the photo he took.

"Well, I'll be. Good thinking, Cassandra. There is a driveway leading nowhere." I was surprised Lara and Lorenzo hadn't remembered it being there.

"Not nowhere," Cassandra said. "It leads to a garage, albeit an invisible one."

"Let's hope, but why do we need to wait for the food delivery person to arrive?" I asked. My mind wasn't as sharp as it usually was.

"Whoever delivers the food would be a trusted person," Daniel said. "They would be in the inner circle. Because they would be guilty of knowingly harboring kidnapped victims, we might be able to make a deal with them for a reduced sentence if they give us the name of their leader."

"I like it, but it could be days before the food truck arrives," I said.

Iggy looked over at Hugo. "Okay, I'll tell them. Hugo said that he can stand watch. When it drives in, he can tell us."

Gavin relayed the information to Daniel. "We can't mobilize my law enforcement friends that quickly."

"If we could be on the property when the driver arrives, that would help," I said, "though that might take days. Ugh."

"Grandma, how long will it take you to summon the dead and do the spell?"

She smiled. "Maybe fifteen seconds."

That part was good. "Let's say we are all in place when this delivery truck arrives. Cassandra then summons the dead who do their thing, resulting in the building appearing and any alarm system or electric fence being deactivated. Then what happens?"

"Then I halt all but the victims, and your men escort them to safety," she said.

That sounded too easy. "What about a bus to transport them? And where would we take so many people?"

"You could have them go to the hotel," Bella said.

"If we did that, the whole town would know what happened," I said.

"Rihanna is right," Lorenzo said. "Do we want to expose the fact that vampires exist? Many of my kind are good people, though sadly many are not. If their existence is known, the vampires might be bolder in their attempts to find blood."

Gavin translated to Daniel. "What Lorenzo said makes sense."

"Let me ask my friends. They might know where the captives can go without much notice."

"Do you think they will want to return to their homes in Netwood?" I asked.

"How about we free them first, have them medically checked out, and then worry about what happens next?" Daniel said.

I blew out a breath. "That sounds good. What's the first step? Will you round up the troops?"

"I can do that," he said.

"Maybe you could ask a few of them to come here so that we can convince them that vampires and other entities are real."

Daniel groaned. "As much as I don't think it will go over well, it might disturb them more to see a building suddenly appear out of thin air. They will be more prepared if they see, say, Hugo appear and disappear."

"I agree."

Daniel nodded. "I'll make the call."

I mouthed to Gavin that I was starving. He turned to Cassandra. "While we wait for Daniel's friends to arrive,

Rihanna and I are going to grab a bite to eat. Would you like to join us?"

"That is very kind of you, but I'd like to spend what time I have with my granddaughter."

"I understand. We'll be downstairs in the hotel restaurant should you need us."

As soon as we left the room, my nerves shot up. "Are we crazy?"

Gavin rubbed his chin. "Are we?"

"I'm serious. What if something goes wrong?"

"We have magic on our side," he said.

"That's my line!" I sucked in a breath. "I just realized those in charge can't be vampires."

"Why not?"

"Vampires don't do spells, which is something that would be needed to cloak the building. Only magic can do that."

His brows pressed together. "Is being held captive by witches any better than vampires?"

"In this case it is. I wouldn't want to be bitten before we had a chance to be rescued."

We took the elevator down two floors to the restaurant, which thankfully wasn't busy.

The waitress showed us to a table. "Coffee?" she asked.

"Most definitely."

Gavin held up a finger. "The safest thing would be not to get caught in the first place, which means we should stay here and let the experts do their thing."

"No way. I want to watch whoever did this to these people be brought to justice. Most likely, these same people killed Lara."

"Is it possible for Hugo to keep us cloaked?"

"Sure, but we could be at the site for hours, which will be cold. And what about the law officers? They'd need to be cloaked too."

He shrugged. "I don't understand Hugo's abilities, but from what I can tell, all he needs to do is touch something and it will be cloaked."

My mind raced. "Yes! That's it. We could rent a van to hold us and the lawmen. If Hugo is inside—or is standing next to the vehicle— maybe he can cloak all of us at the same time."

"It's worth asking him."

The waitress returned with our coffee and took our order. "What are your thoughts about who ran Lara off the road?" I asked once she was out of earshot.

Gavin chuckled. "Like I would know?"

"No, but you can guess."

"Considering some witch or warlock is involved in kidnapping the bitten people, I'd say someone is very serious about keeping the existence of vampires a secret. As to who ran Lara off the road? I'd have to say a person of magic."

"I agree, but that doesn't narrow it down much."

Our food arrived, and we ate quickly since I didn't think it would take long for Daniel to gather a few of his friends. We'd almost finished when Hugo came into the restaurant. The fact he actually walked in instead of teleported said a lot.

"Are Daniel's men in the room?" I asked.

Hugo nodded.

Gavin placed a hand on mine. "You go up and explain what's happening, and I'll flag the waitress and pay."

"Thanks. I don't want to keep them waiting longer than needed."

Hugo and I left. As soon as we were in the elevator, he touched my arm and teleported me into the room. While it was faster for sure, a little notice would have been nice.

The wide eyes and drawn guns had me raising my arms. "I'm Rihanna. Sorry to scare you."

"This is the woman I told you about," Daniel said.

They holstered their guns. "How did you get in here?" the taller of the two officers asked.

Daniel held up a hand. Apparently, he wanted to answer. "I told you. These people have powers that we can't fathom."

"I see."

From his racing thoughts, the lawman didn't see much. "Did Daniel explain what we needed you to do?" I asked.

"He explained it, but I don't believe it," said the officer, "or understand it."

"I have a plan." I sat down and told them about the van. "Hugo, you can cloak it, right?"

He nodded.

"Are you saying we can become invisible while we wait for someone to show up?" the second man asked.

"Yes. Would you like to see this building and what you are up against?"

"Sure."

I explained to both men that Hugo could teleport them to the outside of the building and then take them inside. They needed to make sure not to break contact with Hugo. If they talked, they would be heard. "It's not scary or painful, just kind of creepy."

Both men moved over to Hugo. "We're ready."

I bet they weren't. One minute, they were there, and the next not.

Cassandra Maurel pulled out a few charms and a bag of what I guessed contained some kind of potion. "I need to be ready in case we have to move quickly."

"Good idea. Daniel, did you mention to your lawmen friends that Cassandra would keep the guards immobilized while they moved out the captives?"

"Yes, but even I have a hard time understanding how it works," Daniel said.

"I hear you. Cassandra, when you summon the dead, will we see them?"

She smiled. "Not if I don't want you to."

I kind of smiled. "I think it will be for the best if we don't. You do your thing, and when we see the building appear, we'll give you a minute to take care of the guards, and then our lawmen will go in and arrest those involved."

"Perfect. My *friends* will be very happy to have something more to do. Wielding power provides them with quite a high."

Who knew?

Gavin returned. "What did I miss?"

"A lot." I explained that Hugo was giving the two lawmen a tour of the facility.

As if they'd heard me, Hugo appeared with the officers in tow. Their body language told me they were a bit disoriented, and their minds were racing.

The taller of the two blew out a breath. "We need to hire Hugo. We could catch so many people."

We all laughed.

"On that note, when will you all be ready to do this?"

"Just as soon as the van arrives," Daniel said.

chapter nineteen

"WE'VE BEEN WAITING HERE an hour and no one has shown up." I shouldn't be complaining, but I wasn't used to just sitting and doing nothing. "I don't know how cops do stakeout duty. That would drive me crazy."

Gavin clasped my hand. "It's hard, I know, especially since we are staring at an empty parking lot."

I wanted to ask Cassandra when she planned to start her spell, but I had to trust she knew what she was doing. Thankfully, Bella, Lara, and Lorenzo were inside making sure nothing had changed. I'm sure Hugo wanted to go in and check on them, but he needed to keep a hand on the van so we didn't appear.

Both of the officers sat up. "I hear an engine."

I did, too, but it could be a passing car.

When a white van pulled up, Cassandra pushed open the passenger side door. She lifted a hand. "Don't worry about me. I can cloak myself."

With that promise, she stepped outside—or so I assumed since I couldn't see her.

I had no idea what she was going to do exactly, and that

frustrated me. To be able to see a voodoo priestess in action would have been fantastic.

Daniel, who'd driven our vehicle, had a pair of binoculars trained on the van that was idling in the driveway. "I think I see one of those vampire slayer stickers like the one Lorenzo described on the bumper."

That was encouraging, as it was better to be dealing with a vampire slayer than a vampire. A moment later, the van pulled forward and disappeared into the building. I waited for the building to appear, but it didn't.

I leaned over to Gavin. "I thought Cassandra said it would only take fifteen seconds to summon her people."

He kissed my cheek. "Trust her."

As if my words had floated out to the universe, the building appeared and so did Cassandra. I searched for the scores of helpers, but saw no one. Darn.

A moment after she entered the building, the two lawmen rushed out of our van. I guess it didn't matter now if anyone saw them since Cassandra would be *freezing* the men carrying guns.

As the men made their way to the building, one of the officers pulled out a phone and made a call. They had a bus and several other officers down the road out of sight, waiting to be told the coast was clear.

Gavin clasped my hand. "Don't even think about it."

"Think about what?"

"You know. Going in there. The lawmen have enough to deal with physically and emotionally. They don't need to be watching out for you."

He was right. A moment later, three police cars, followed by a bus, pulled into the lot. That helped calm me a bit. With guns drawn—which weren't necessary—they rushed into the building. What seemed like forever later, the first of the hostages were led outside to the bus. Yes!

"I need some information," I said. "Coming? It's safe."

He smiled. "Do I have a choice?"

"Always. Though not in this case." I blew him a kiss.

While I wanted to ask each of them a million questions, I'm sure they had more questions about what just happened than I did. Cassandra might be the best person to explain it to them once she was free to chat.

Gavin and I waited outside the bus until the hostages had a chance to settle in. I doubt they were told where they would be going, but I bet they didn't care. Free was free.

Next, several men were escorted outside in cuffs, as well as one woman. I didn't remember seeing any females when I did my quick search of the encampment with Hugo, but she could have been in an office.

Not able to contain my curiosity any longer, I stepped onto the bus and spoke to a woman in the front seat. "Excuse me, but do you know who that woman is?" I nodded to the lady being escorted to a police vehicle.

She huffed. "Boy, do I. That's Vicky Schlemmer."

Schlemmer? "Is she related to Sheriff Schlemmer?"

"Yes. She's his wife."

"His wife? What is she doing here?"

The woman huffed. "She was holding us captive."

The sheriff's wife was responsible for this atrocity? "Why? Did she think you all would tell the world about vampires?"

The woman's eyes widened. "You know about them?"

"Yes." They must have been told the truth about the bite marks, or else they figured it out.

"Were you bitten by one?" the woman asked.

"No, but I know about them. Not all are bad. Be thankful the ones here didn't kill you."

She nodded. "I know, but if we told people, the whole town might freak and move. That would be terrible for our livelihood."

Yikes. This woman sounded like she almost agreed with Vicky Schlemmer. "Aren't you angry that your life was basically taken away from you?"

"Of course, but just because I understood why Vicky and her husband wanted to keep things quiet, doesn't mean I agreed with their methods."

So the sheriff was involved. "Did you hear that a vampire killed the sheriff?" Okay, I wasn't positive that was how he died, but Lorenzo believed it.

"No, though I can't say I'm sad about it." She leaned closer. "Do you know what they are going to do with us now?"

"I think they had planned to have you all checked out medically. Then? I don't know other than you will be safe."

Daniel stepped into the bus. "We need to go," he said to me.

"Okay." I turned back to the woman. "Good luck."

"Thank you."

We returned to the van. "Where's Cassandra?" I asked.

"Hugo escorted her back to New Orleans."

Darn. I wanted to ask her questions about how she managed to *freeze* some people while allowing others to move about. Hopefully, Bella could fill me in.

Seconds later Bella, Lara, and Lorenzo appeared in the van.

Bella smiled. "I told you my grandmother was something."

"She was more than something. She was amazing. Were you able to see those she summoned?" I asked.

"Yes. There were about twenty of them. They stood in a line, lifted their hands, and chanted something I didn't understand. A moment later the building appeared. The dead knew what to do, because they floated inside. Of course, I followed. I figured the guards didn't have a chance when the dead surrounded them."

"Do you know how your grandmother was able to keep the guards at bay?"

"I wish," Bella huffed.

Too bad.

"How did they know there weren't other guards in the facility?" Gavin asked.

"A few left the group and searched all of the rooms. We are a fast bunch, you know."

I smiled. "I'm just thrilled that it all worked out."

"What about my murder?" Lara asked.

I was wondering when she'd ask that question. "Let's give Daniel's lawmen a chance to figure things out."

Daniel took off, and we were back at the hotel in no time. "Guys, I need to return the van, and then I want to check up on things," he said.

I understood. "Of course. Thank you for everything. We couldn't have done this without you."

"No, thank you. You gave me closure—or rather more closure. Now, I need answers about Lara's death."

"You and us both." We climbed out of the van and went up to the room since I wanted to speak with our ghostly friends in private. When we opened the door, Hugo was there communicating with Iggy.

"Did Cassandra get back okay?" I asked.

Hugo nodded.

I turned to the others. "After a few hours of sitting, I need some food, so why don't you all stay here for a bit and fill Iggy in on the adventure? We won't be long."

"Sure," Lara said.

The glance between her and Lorenzo told me they were up to something. At the moment, I was willing to let them do their thing. "I hope Daniel realizes that Vicky Schlemmer—or someone she hired—is a powerful witch or warlock. The cops need to be careful of her."

Lara looked over at Hugo. “Maybe the four of us should make sure she doesn’t pull a fast one.”

“How do you know where they are?”

If they hadn’t all disappeared at once, they might have answered.

“I didn’t get to hear all the details,” Iggy said.

“I promise we will fill you in as soon as we return from eating. Let’s say that we caught the bad guy.”

“Who was it?”

“The sheriff’s wife. And I don’t know more than that. Maybe Hugo can fill you in when they get back.”

“Whatever.”

Oh no. He was picking up some of Bella’s mannerisms.

We left, and true to our word, we weren’t gone long. When Gavin and I returned from the diner, Daniel was waiting for us in the lobby.

“I have news,” he said.

“Come on up to the room.”

When we entered, everyone was there with smiles on their faces, which implied they’d done something. I’d deal with them later.

Gavin motioned Daniel take a seat. “I don’t know where to begin,” he said. “I normally consider myself a well-rounded man who is open to new ideas.”

“You are! You now believe in ghosts, teleporting gargoyle shifters, and voodoo magic.”

He smiled. “I guess you are right.”

“What did you learn?” Gavin asked.

“Some of the guards folded once we told them they would face many years in jail unless they cooperated. They told us that they were hired to guard who they thought were enemies of the state. In fact, they were told that all of the people in the converted orphanage were the vampires, not the victims of vampires.”

I dipped my chin. "Did you believe them?"

Bella flew to the table. "That's the truth. Just ask Hugo."

I looked around. "Iggy, where are you? We need your expertise."

He waddled out from under the bed, but he still wasn't all that happy with us. I suspected he was upset that he missed out on all of the theatrics in taking down Vicky Schlemmer and her group even though it would have meant he'd have had to sit in a cold van for a while.

He looked over at Hugo, nodded a few times, and then came over to the table. I picked him up and placed him in front of us. "Tell me, and I'll translate."

"Hugo placed his hands on the side of a few of the guards' heads. They did think they were guarding vampires."

I told Daniel what Iggy said.

"Hugo, or anyone, do you know if the guards are members of the vampire slayer society, or whatever it is officially called?" Daniel said.

Since Hugo was the only one besides Iggy that we could see, he nodded.

"Oh, we forgot to tell you the best part," Lara said.

"What is that?"

"Lorenzo found out that Vicky ran me off the road."

"What?"

Gavin told Daniel.

"Ask Lara how he found out?" Daniel said.

Of course, she could hear him, so I didn't need to repeat it. Lara moved out of the way and let Lorenzo take center stage. "I knew you wouldn't have approved, but I needed to know for myself. I probed Vicky's mind. I had to hypnotize her for a minute so she'd allow me to read her thoughts."

"Maybe you can teach me that trick," I said.

He smiled. "You'd have to have vampire blood in you, and I don't think you'd like the side effects."

"True. So what did Vicky say?"

Gavin whispered the conversation to Daniel. He pulled out his phone. "Mind if I record what you say, Gavin. No, I can't use it in a court of law, but having this knowledge might help me."

"Sure."

"Lorenzo, go on. What did Vicky do?" I prompted.

"As we know, Lara found the album in her father-in-law's attic. Perplexed what it contained, she showed it to her nail tech."

"Because Becca was into the occult stuff. I remember that," I said.

"Yes. Apparently, she told her husband about it. And guess what? He's a member of this secret voodoo slayer society."

"Don't tell me the husband told the sheriff who told his wife?" I asked.

"Yes. Sheriff Schlemmer headed this group. Vicky didn't want to see her husband's life mission be destroyed by what Lara found, so she took it upon herself to silence Lara."

Gavin dictated the information into the phone's recorder.

Daniel whistled. "This is incredible. Ask Lara the name of her nail tech."

"It's Becca Nations, but I bet she'll deny everything, especially if her husband is a member of this society."

"Hang them all," Iggy shouted.

I laughed. "Iggy, what has gotten into you? That's not the way we do things. You know that. I'm sure Daniel will make sure that the people who held all those victims captive are brought to justice."

"I will. As for Lara's murder, I'll make sure the District Attorney's do their job and prosecute Vicky Schlemmer."

"Do you really think a jury will buy into the existence of vampires?" I asked. "If not, Vicky will say everyone is crazy."

"I fear that might happen. I'm hoping there is some evidence on her car bumper that she rammed Lara's car."

"It's at Jake's auto—or at least it was." I told Daniel about the phone call. "Jake might have had have it towed someplace and destroyed."

"That would be bad," Daniel said.

"I could ask some of my relatives to come up here and do a demonstration of vampires and how they can bite a person if that would help a jury decide," Lorenzo offered.

"Would you have them hypnotize the jury and then suck out their blood to prove vampires are real?" I hoped not.

Daniel chuckled. I guess he didn't need to hear Lorenzo's comment.

"If you'd like," Lorenzo said.

I turned to Daniel and explained Lorenzo's offer. "He is just trying to help."

"Lorenzo, I appreciate it, but we'll use the law to prosecute these people."

Lara moved next to Daniel. "Do you think he can get the case against Vicky to stick?" she asked.

I doubted it. "Let's hope, but at least you know who killed you and why."

Lara floated to the ground and seemed to sit. "I wonder if James was a part of this society. Maybe that's why he didn't fight very hard to find out who ran me over."

"I wouldn't be surprised," I said.

Iggy faced me. "What about poor Cameron? What are you going to tell him?"

I looked over at Daniel. "Do you think you can talk to Cameron? I know he'd like closure."

"When I know a bit more, I will definitely fill him in."

I stood and walked over to the safe. "You should have this album. It will go a long way in helping to convict Vicky and the others of kidnapping. At least she'll be going to jail for that offense."

I opened the safe, took out the book, and then handed it to Daniel.

"Thank you, Rihanna and Gavin, for helping me come to grips with my loss." He looked around. "And a big thank you to Hugo, Lara, Bella, and Lorenzo. Someday, I hope we will meet again."

"Eww," Iggy said. "Then you'll be dead."

I didn't translate that. "Just worry about yourself, young man." I looked over at Hugo. "Can you take my dissatisfied little one home?"

Hugo smiled, picked up Iggy, and disappeared.

Daniel whistled. "When I wake up tomorrow, I wonder if I'll think this has all been a dream."

"I totally understand," I said. "It is difficult to grasp."

Daniel pushed back his chair. "Lara, wherever you are, I miss you and will never forget you."

She slowly floated through him. When he shivered, I was happy to know he felt her. "Tell him, I love him."

"Lara says that she loves you."

I swear, Daniel's eyes watered. He held out his hand to me. "Thank you, again."

"You bet."

Once Daniel left, I went over to the bed and dropped down. Mentally, I was quite tired. "We'll need to make airline reservations."

"Do we?" he asked.

"What do you mean?"

"You could ask your cousin to ask Hugo to escort us back?"

"I like that idea. It will be so much faster."

The three amigos floated in front of us. "This time, I want

to say goodbye properly," Bella said. "The last time, I just ran off."

"I remember."

Bella flew over and kind of hugged me. "Thank you."

Next came Lara and then Lorenzo. "If you are ever in New Orleans," he said. "Just give me a shout."

"Is that how it works?"

"I don't know, but I bet Bella's grandma could help you out."

I smiled. "I bet she could."

The three disappeared, and I faced Gavin. "Maybe we could rest tonight and find our way home tomorrow."

"That is the best idea you've had yet."

I had to say, my first two sleuth cases turned out pretty well, but taking photos was so much easier.

I hope you enjoyed another Rihanna adventure with Bella and Lorenzo. Next up is GHOSTS JUST WANT TO HAVE FUN.

An innocent photo outing, a very stiff dead body, and more surprises than the words in a song.

Wouldn't you know it? The one time my cousin, Glinda, and her fiancé, decide to go camping (I know right), I stumble upon a dead body in some abandon farm house. Turns out the guy was some famous singer who quit the music business ten years ago.

I would have let the sheriff handle the investigation, except that the body was in a rather strange condition, which implied magic was involved. That's where I come in. Okay, the sheriff really wanted my cousin to help since she is a sleuth and a witch, but she wasn't in town, so guess what? I was asked to help investigate. Yes, I'm a witch too, but my talents extend mostly to mind reading and an occasional séance.

No murder mystery would be complete without Iggy, and a few other helpers—like my ghost friends Bella and Lorenzo. If you want to see how we solved the crime, just come to the Pink Iguana Sleuths' office in Witch's Cove, Florida to chat.

Here is the first chapter:

"I can't believe it's time for you to go." I pressed my lips into a pout.

My cousin, Glinda Goodall, hugged me. "Jaxson and I won't be gone *that* long."

"I hope not, but a week seems like forever." Though, if the weather didn't cooperate, they might return sooner. I still didn't understand why they decided to go hiking in North Carolina since Glinda disliked all forms of exercise, and climbing mountains would be a lot of work. "You do know that camping won't be easy, right?" I didn't let her answer. "Have you ever hung a bear bag, pumped water, or started a fire?"

"That's what my fiancé is for." Glinda looked up at Jaxson and grinned.

"I told her that I'm expecting her to help. Glinda can pump the water and maybe cook."

I swallowed a laugh. I'd love to be a fly on that tree watching Glinda navigate the out of doors. Jaxson was the one who loved traipsing around in the woods, and I trusted him completely to keep her safe. But camping? I worried she would be miserable. "I hope you have a fabulous time."

"I plan to." Glinda looked over at Iggy, her talking pink iguana familiar. "And you, mister, better behave and do what

Rihanna tells you to do. No flowers for a month if she says you sassed her or snuck out when you weren't supposed to."

The iguana lifted his head. "How is that fair?"

Glinda stood up taller. "Are you saying you'd rather go camping with us instead of being cooped up here?"

My cousin had warned Iggy about the possibility of a bear sighting, not to mention how the nights could dip into the thirties or forties in the mountains. Temperatures that cold might kill the cold-blooded reptile.

"No. Just go." He turned around and waddled under the sofa, his favorite hiding place.

Just as they were about to leave, someone knocked on the Pink Iguana Sleuths' office door.

"That must be Nicky." I thought she was stopping by in an hour. Either I misunderstood her, or Nicky had the time wrong. I voted for the latter. Keeping an accurate calendar wasn't Nicky's strong point.

"Who's Nicky?" Jaxson asked, sounding rather protective.

"Didn't I mention her? We are in the same photo class together, and we have a class project to do. We're going to work on that today."

Glinda smiled. "I think that's wonderful."

I pulled open the door and motioned her in. Nicky stopped. "Oh. I thought you said your cousin was on vacation."

"They're just leaving." I introduced them.

Iggy came out from under the sofa. "Hi."

Nicky looked over at him. "So you're Iggy. Rihanna has told me all about you. Nice to meet you."

"You can hear me?"

She grinned. "Yes. I have witch powers. Rihanna didn't mention that?"

"No. She doesn't tell me anything." With that announcement, he turned around and went back to his hiding place.

Nicky chuckled. "You said he was sassy."

"He is at that," I threw back.

"Don't mind my familiar," Glinda said. "He's mad because we are going camping up North, and he can't go. It's too cold and probably too dangerous for him."

"Well, don't worry. Rihanna and I will take good care of him."

Really? I thought she was only planning to stay for an afternoon.

"Thank you." Glinda hugged me again, and then she and Jaxson finally headed out.

"Have fun!" I called.

Once they were gone, I motioned for Nicky to take a seat. "So where do you want to take pictures?"

The assignment was all things vintage—as in old.

"Well, I've been doing a little reconnaissance of the area. A couple of miles from here is an abandoned farm house that would be wonderful to photograph."

Since I'd only moved to Witch's Cove, Florida two and a half years ago, I wasn't familiar with every nook and cranny of the area. "Sounds perfect. Let me grab my camera."

After I stuffed a few bottles of water in my backpack, I bent down to find Iggy. He slowly crawled out. "Do you want to come with us?"

"Do you have food for me?"

Iggy was always hungry. "I can pack a container of lettuce, but we'll be outside, so there's always leaves for you to munch on, you know."

"Yeah, but I like lettuce better."

"I'll pack some for you then." I guess that meant he wanted to join us, though I wasn't sure why he wanted to go. Maybe he was a little out of sorts now that Glinda and Jaxson were gone.

It wasn't as if he couldn't come and go as he pleased,

however. There was a cat door he used all the time, and he had no shortage of friends he could visit. Some were of the animal variety while others were gargoyle shifters.

I placed a few pieces of lettuce in a container and jammed it into my backpack. I looked over at Nicky whose backpack wasn't very full. "Do you mind carrying Iggy?"

"Not at all."

She picked him up and let him ride on top of her pack. When he didn't complain, we took off. I drove while Nicky navigated since she had seen the place from the road and knew where we were going—more or less.

After following her directions for a while, Nicky pointed to a poorly paved road. I turned right down it and had to hold the wheel tightly to avoid being bumped all over the place.

"Hey, watch it," Iggy said, clearly not happy with the road conditions.

"I have no control over the ruts in the road."

"You could drive slower."

Smart aleck. I did let up on the gas a little.

Nicky picked him up and held him, which would be more secure.

"It's over there." She sounded quite excited.

I slowed. "It sure looks abandoned, what with the roof half caved in."

No one seemed to be about. Good. We certainly didn't need to be questioned by the sheriff should someone see us and call it in, though Steve Rocker knew Glinda and me very well. Worst case, he'd tell me not to enter a property without permission in the future.

I cut the engine, grabbed my pack from the back seat, and slid out. The day was really warm, but thankfully there was a slight breeze to keep us from overheating.

Since the property wasn't fenced, it made for easy access to the house. The best part was that the nearest neighbor was a football field away. I didn't see any cars in their drive, and from the lack of care, the homestead might be empty too.

"I wasn't thinking when I dressed this morning. I didn't wear the right shoes for this excursion," Nicky said.

The grass hadn't been cut in a long time, and since Nicky had on backless sandals, it would make walking around a little difficult. At least I had worn sneakers. "How about we take pictures from the street to start?"

"Good idea."

"What about me?" Iggy asked.

"What about you? Do you want to wander on your own?" No one was about, so Iggy couldn't get into too much trouble, assuming he didn't mind forging through the weeds. "I hope there are no snakes in the grass."

He lifted his head. "How about I ride on the top of your backpack? It will be safer up there."

I smiled. "Sure." I lifted Iggy from Nicky's pack, though he would have been safe with her too.

I went left and Nicky headed right. It was always fun to compare the different photos at day's end. I took a few shots of the front of the house and then traipsed down the side of the property where the grass was dying. Because it was matted down, it made walking easier.

"Someone's in the back of the house," Iggy announced. "Maybe we should leave."

I squinted but saw no one. "Where do you see someone?"

"I told you. In the house. I have eagle eyes, remember? Or rather lizard eyes."

Iggy could see and hear better than I could. "Are you sure it's a person though? No one should be in there. The house is missing half the roof, and most of the windows are broken."

"It's a person, but he's not moving."

That was strange. "I'll check it out when I get over there."

"Hurry." Iggy crawled up the strap of the backpack and sat

on my shoulder, making it hard for me to lift my arm to take any pictures. He might be a lot of things, but he wasn't this demanding without a reason—at least not usually.

"Fine. Which window is it?"

"The back one."

I wanted to move closer to the structure anyway, and this was a good excuse to do so.

I called out to Nicky, and she waved back. "Iggy said he sees something inside." I motioned I was going in, and Nicky nodded.

As I waded through the tall grass and around the overgrown shrubs, I had to step around beer bottles, rocks, paper products, and a host of other unsavory items. I had the sense this place might have been used as a hangout for the teenage crowd.

Okay, technically I was a teenager since I was only nineteen, but I had to grow up faster than most once my dad died. I take that back—once my alcoholic mother told me at the age of three that my father was dead. Truth was, he was an undercover FBI agent who didn't want the world to know we existed for fear someone would harm us. Regardless of the reason, it was just me and my mom, though I was lucky enough to meet him last year—right before he was murdered.

As long as I'm spilling my guts here, I might as well introduce myself. I'm Rihanna Samuels. I moved into the back room of my cousin's office when Mom went into rehab. And the rest is history as they say, other than the fact I have a real hunky boyfriend, Gavin Sanchez, but he's away at college studying to be a doctor.

Iggy lifted his claw as if to point. "Do you see him?"

My heart stilled. A very stiff man was sitting upright in a chair, looking rather...dead. "Oh, my. Maybe it's a mannequin."

Iggy sniffed. "Nope. He's dead. You know how much I

hate the smell of death. When Glinda or you visit the morgue, you reek. And I can smell real good, remember?"

Yes, he could, though I smelled nothing. "Let's see if we can get inside."

"Are you kidding? Leave me out here."

I glanced to the lizard on my shoulder. "I need someone to protect me."

"Then contact Hugo."

Excluding Iggy's immediate human family, Hugo was Iggy's best friend. The gargoyle shifter might be mute, but he had a lot of powers. Teleporting was just one of his abilities as was temporarily paralyzing someone. "I don't think a dead man can harm me."

Iggy lifted his claw to his snout, which was his version of a face plant. "The person who killed the guy could still be in the house."

I lifted him off my shoulder so I could see him better. "Why do you think he was murdered?"

Iggy opened his mouth and then shut it.

"I thought so," I shot back. "Come on."

If I believed we were in any kind of danger, I would have contacted Hugo. I stopped, letting reason sink in. At the very least, it might be smart to let someone know where we were in case anything happened to us.

Since Genevieve, another gargoyle shifter, was Hugo's girlfriend, I called her. Hugo being mute didn't do well using a phone.

She answered right away. "Hey, did Glinda and Jaxson leave?"

"Yes, about a half hour ago. I just wanted to let you know that my friend Nicky and I are at an abandoned house taking pictures, and that Iggy spotted what I think is a dead guy inside."

"Oh, no. Where are you?"

I didn't want to bother Genevieve, but she too could teleport, so I told her the approximate location.

"We'll be right there."

I didn't have the chance to even say she didn't need to come when both Hugo and Genevieve showed up. I swear she must have secretly implanted a GPS chip under my skin since she and Hugo always could find me.

"You came!" Iggy shouted.

Hugo smiled and removed Iggy from my grasp. Those two had such a special bond.

"Where is this guy?" she asked.

I guess her sense of smell wasn't as good as Iggy's either. "In the back of the house."

The three of them disappeared. Now that those two had arrived, it was probably safer inside than out.

Nicky picked her way over to me. "Who were you talking to just now?"

I explained about the two teleporting shifters. Because Nicky was a witch, she seemed to take their existence in stride. I had to say, she did better than I did when I first met those two. Changing from an animal into a human almost seemed normal to me, but stone to flesh? That was a totally different thing.

"Hugo and Genevieve are checking out the inside to make sure it's safe."

"From the roof collapsing?"

I guess I forgot to mention that real reason. "No from the dead guy inside—or rather from someone who might have killed him. That's assuming it's not a very lifelike mannequin. Though if it were, Genevieve and Hugo would have come out and told me by now."

"Oh, my. Did you call the sheriff?"

In my surprise at seeing the body—or what I believed was a body, I'd completely forgotten the protocol. Considering my boyfriend's mother was the town's medical examiner, I should have remembered. "I'll do that now."

It seemed even strange to me that I had the sheriff's office on speed dial, but I did.

Pearl Dillsmith, the sheriff's aging grandmother and dispatcher, answered. "Witch's Cove sheriff's department. How can I help you?"

She usually recognized my cell phone number. Pearl must be distracted. "Hey, Pearl, it's Rihanna. I'm afraid I found a dead body or rather Iggy did."

excerpt—ghosts just want to have fun

Don't forget to sign up for my Cozy Mystery newsletter *to learn about my discounts and upcoming releases. If you prefer to only receive notices regarding my releases, follow me on BookBub.*

Here is a sneak peek of book 3: GHOSTS JUST WANT TO HAVE FUN.

An innocent photo outing, a very stiff dead body, and more surprises than the words in a song.

Wouldn't you know it? The one time my cousin, Glinda, and her fiancé, decide to go camping (I know right), I stumble upon a dead body in some abandon farm house. Turns out the guy was some famous singer who quit the music business ten years ago.

I would have let the sheriff handle the investigation, except that the body was in a rather strange condition, which implied magic was involved. That's where I come in. Okay, the sheriff really wanted my cousin to help since she is a sleuth and a witch, but she wasn't in town, so guess what? I was asked to help investigate. Yes, I'm a witch too, but my talents extend mostly to mind reading and an occasional séance.

No murder mystery would be complete without Iggy, and a few other helpers—like my ghost friends Bella and Lorenzo. If you want to see how we solved the crime, just come to the Pink Iguana Sleuths' office in Witch's Cove, Florida to chat.

Here is the first chapter:

"I can't believe it's time for you to go." I pressed my lips into a pout.

My cousin, Glinda Goodall, hugged me. "Jaxson and I won't be gone *that* long."

"I hope not, but a week seems like forever." Though, if the weather didn't cooperate, they might return sooner. I still didn't understand why they decided to go camping and hiking in North Carolina since Glinda disliked all forms of exercise, and climbing mountains would be a lot of work. "Have you ever hung a bear bag, pumped water, or started a fire?"

"That's what my fiancé is for." Glinda looked up at Jaxson and grinned.

"I told her that I'm expecting her to help. Glinda can pump the water and maybe cook."

I swallowed a laugh. I'd love to be a fly on that tree watching Glinda navigate the out of doors. Jaxson was the one who loved traipsing around in the woods, and I trusted him completely to keep her safe. But camping? I worried she would be miserable. "I hope you have a fabulous time."

"I plan to." Glinda looked over at Iggy, her talking pink iguana familiar. "And you, mister, better behave and do what Rihanna tells you to do. No flowers for a month if she says you sassed her or snuck out when you weren't supposed to."

The iguana lifted his head. "How is that fair?"

Glinda stood up straighter. "Are you saying you'd rather go camping with us instead of being cooped up here?"

My cousin had warned Iggy about the possibility of a bear

sighting, not to mention how the nights could dip into the thirties or forties in the mountains. Temperatures that cold might kill the cold-blooded reptile.

"No. Just go." He turned around and waddled under the sofa, his favorite hiding place.

Just as they were about to leave, someone knocked on the Pink Iguana Sleuths' office door.

"That must be Nicky." I thought she was stopping by in an hour. Either I misunderstood her, or Nicky had the time wrong. I voted for the latter. Keeping an accurate calendar wasn't Nicky's strong point.

"Who's Nicky?" Jaxson asked, sounding rather protective.

"Nicky Andrews and I are in the same photo class together, and we have a class project to do. We're going to work on that today."

Glinda smiled. "I think that's wonderful."

I pulled open the door and motioned her in. Nicky entered and then stopped. "Oh. I thought you said your cousin was on vacation."

"They're just leaving." I introduced them.

Iggy came out from under the sofa. "Hi, I'm Iggy."

Nicky looked over at him. "Iggy, Rihanna has told me all about you. Nice to meet you."

"You can hear me?"

She grinned. "Yes. I have witch powers. Rihanna didn't mention that?"

"No. She doesn't tell me anything." With that announcement, he turned around and went back to his hiding place.

Nicky chuckled. "You said he was sassy."

"He is at that," I threw back.

"Don't mind my familiar," Glinda said. "He's mad because we are going camping up North, and he can't go. It's too cold and probably too dangerous for him."

"Well, don't worry. Rihanna and I will take good care of him."

Really? I thought she was only planning to stay for an afternoon.

"Thank you." Glinda hugged me again, and then she and Jaxson finally headed out.

"Have fun!" I called.

Once they were gone, I motioned for Nicky to take a seat. "So where do you want to take pictures?"

The assignment was all things vintage—as in old.

"Well, I've been doing a little reconnaissance of the area. A couple of miles from here is an abandoned farm house that would be wonderful to photograph."

Since I'd only moved to Witch's Cove, Florida two and a half years ago, I wasn't familiar with every nook and cranny of the area. "Sounds perfect. Let me grab my camera."

After I stuffed a few bottles of water in my backpack, I bent down to find Iggy. "Do you want to come with us?"

He slowly crawled out. "Do you have food for me?"

Iggy was always hungry. "I can pack a container of lettuce, but we'll be outside, so there's always leaves for you to munch on, you know."

"Yeah, but I like lettuce better."

"I'll pack some for you then." I guess that meant he wanted to join us, though I wasn't sure why he wanted to go. Maybe he was a little out of sorts now that Glinda and Jaxson were gone.

It wasn't as if he couldn't come and go as he pleased if he stayed here, however. There was a cat door he used all the time, and he had no shortage of friends he could visit. Some were of the animal variety while others were gargoyle shifters.

I placed a few pieces of lettuce in a container that I jammed it into my backpack. I looked over at Nicky. "Do you mind carrying Iggy?"

"Not at all."

She picked him up and let him ride on top of her pack. When he didn't complain, we took off. I drove while Nicky navigated since she had seen the place from the road and knew where we were going—more or less.

After following her directions for a while, Nicky pointed to a poorly paved road. I turned right down it and had to hold the wheel tightly to avoid being bumped all over the place.

"Hey, watch it," Iggy said, clearly not happy with the road conditions.

"I have no control over the ruts in the road."

"You could drive slower."

Smart aleck. I did let up on the gas a little.

Nicky picked him up and held him, which would be more secure.

"It's over there," she said, sounding rather excited that she found the location again.

I slowed. "It sure looks abandoned, what with the roof half caved in."

No one seemed to be about either. Good. We certainly didn't need to be questioned by the sheriff should someone see us and call it in, though Steve Rocker knew Glinda and me very well. Worst case, he'd tell me not to enter a property without permission in the future.

I cut the engine, grabbed my pack from the back seat, and slid out. The day was really warm, but thankfully there was a slight breeze to keep us from overheating.

Since the property wasn't fenced, it made for easy access to the house. The best part was that the nearest neighbor was a football field away. I didn't see any cars in their drive, and from the lack of care, the homestead might be empty too.

Nicky lifted her foot. "I wasn't thinking when I dressed this morning. I didn't wear the right shoes for this excursion."

The grass hadn't been cut in a long time, and since Nicky

had on backless sandals, it would make walking around a little difficult. At least I had worn sneakers. "How about we start by taking pictures from the street?"

"Good idea."

"What about me?" Iggy asked.

"What about you? Do you want to wander on your own?" No one was about, so Iggy couldn't get into too much trouble, assuming he didn't mind forging through the weeds. "I hope there are no snakes in the grass."

He lifted his head. "How about I ride on the top of your backpack? It will be safer up there."

I smiled. "Sure." I lifted Iggy from Nicky's pack, though he would have been safe with her too.

After a few initial shots of the front, I walked left and Nicky headed right. It was always fun to compare the different photos at day's end. I then traipsed down the side of the property where the grass was matted down, as it would be easier to walk there.

"Someone's in the rear of the house," Iggy announced. "Maybe we should leave."

I squinted but saw no one. "Where do you see someone?"

"I told you. In the house. I have eagle eyes, remember? Or rather lizard eyes."

Iggy could see and hear better than I could. "Are you sure it's a person though? No one should be in there. The house is missing half the roof, and most of the windows are broken."

"It's a person, but he's not moving."

That was strange. "I'll check it out when I get over there."

"Hurry." Iggy crawled up the strap of the backpack and sat on my shoulder, making it hard for me to lift my arm to take any pictures. He might be a lot of things, but he wasn't this demanding without a reason—at least not usually.

"Fine. Which window is it?"

"The back one."

I wanted to move closer to the structure anyway, and this was a good excuse to do so.

I called out to Nicky, who walked over to my side of the house and waved. "Find something?"

"Iggy said he sees something inside." I motioned I was going in, and Nicky nodded.

As I waded through the grass and around the overgrown shrubs, I had to step around beer bottles, rocks, paper products, and a host of other unsavory items. I had the sense this place might have been used as a hangout for the teenage crowd.

Okay, technically I was a teenager since I was only nineteen, but I had to grow up faster than most once my dad died. I take that back—once my alcoholic mother told me at the age of three that my father was dead. Truth was, he was an undercover FBI agent who didn't want the world to know we existed for fear someone would harm us. Regardless of the reason, it was just me and my mom, though I was lucky enough to meet my dad last year—right before he was murdered.

As long as I'm spilling my guts here, I might as well introduce myself. I'm Rihanna Samuels. I moved into the back room of my cousin's office when Mom went into rehab. And the rest is history as they say, other than the fact I have a real hunky boyfriend, Gavin Sanchez, who's away at college studying to be a doctor.

Iggy lifted his claw as if to point. "Do you see him?"

My heart stilled. A very stiff looking man was sitting upright in a chair, appearing quite dead. "Oh, my. Maybe it's a mannequin."

Iggy sniffed. "Nope. He's dead. You know how much I hate the smell of death. When Glinda or you visit the morgue, you reek. And I can smell real good, remember?"

Yes, he could, though I smelled nothing. The odor could

be mold coming from inside the abandoned house. "Let's see if we can get inside."

"Are you kidding? Leave me out here."

I glanced to the lizard on my shoulder. "I need someone to protect me."

And yes, I was kidding.

"Then contact Hugo."

Excluding Iggy's immediate human family, Hugo was Iggy's best friend. The gargoyle shifter might be mute, but he had a lot of powers. Teleporting was just one of his abilities as was temporarily paralyzing someone with a touch "I don't think a dead man can harm me."

Iggy lifted his claw to his snout, which was his version of a face plant. "The person who killed the guy could still be in the house."

I lifted him off my shoulder so I could see him better. "Why do you think he was murdered?"

Iggy opened his mouth and then shut it.

"I thought so," I shot back. "Come on."

If I believed we were in any kind of danger, I would have contacted Hugo. I stopped, letting reason sink in. At the very least, it might be smart to let someone know where we were in case we didn't return.

Since Genevieve, another gargoyle shifter, was Hugo's girlfriend, I called her. Hugo, being mute, didn't do well using a phone.

She answered right away. "Hey, did Glinda and Jaxson leave?"

"Yes, about a half hour ago. I just wanted to let you know that my friend Nicky and I are at an abandoned farm house taking pictures. Iggy spotted what I think is a dead guy inside."

"Oh, no. Where are you?"

I didn't want to bother Genevieve, but she too could teleport, so I told her the approximate location.

"We'll be right there."

I didn't have the chance to even say she didn't need to come when both Hugo and Genevieve showed up. I swear she must have secretly implanted a GPS chip under my skin since she and Hugo always could find me.

"You came!" Iggy shouted.

Hugo smiled and removed Iggy from my grasp. Those two had such a special bond.

"Where is this guy?" she asked.

I guess her sense of smell wasn't as good as Iggy's either. "In the rear of the house."

The three of them disappeared. Now that those two had arrived, it was probably safer inside than out.

Nicky picked her way over to me. "Who were you talking to just now?"

I explained about the two teleporting shifters. Because Nicky was a witch, she seemed to take their existence in stride. I had to say, she did better than I did when I first met those two. Changing from an animal into a human almost seemed normal to me, but stone to flesh? That was a totally different thing.

"Hugo and Genevieve are checking out the inside to make sure it's safe."

"From the roof collapsing?"

I guess I forgot to mention the real reason for their sudden appearance. "No from the dead guy inside—or rather from someone who might have killed him. That's assuming it's not a very lifelike mannequin. Though if it were, Genevieve and Hugo would have come out and told me by now."

"Oh, my. Did you call the sheriff?"

In my surprise at seeing the body, I'd completely forgotten the protocol. Considering my boyfriend's mother was the town's medical examiner, I should have remembered. "I'll do that now."

It seemed even strange to me that I had the sheriff's office on speed dial, but I did.

Pearl Dillsmith, the sheriff's aging grandmother and dispatcher, answered. "Witch's Cove sheriff's department. How can I help you?"

She usually recognized my cell phone number. Pearl must have been distracted. "Hey, Pearl, it's Rihanna. I'm afraid I found a dead body—or rather Iggy did."

THE END

about the author

Love it HOT and STEAMY? Sign up for my newsletter and receive MONTANA DESIRE for FREE. Click here

OR Are you a fan of quirky PARANORMAL COZY MYSTERIES? Sign up for this newsletter. Click Here

Not only do I love to read, write, and dream, I'm an extrovert. I enjoy being around people and am always trying to understand what makes them tick. Not only must my romance books have a happily ever after, I need characters I can relate to. My men are wonderful, dynamic, smart, strong, and the best lovers in the world (of course).

My Paranormal Cozy Mysteries are where I let my imagination run wild with witches and a talking pink iguana who believes he's a real sleuth.

I believe I am the luckiest woman. I do what I love and I have a wonderful, supportive husband, who happens to be hot!

Fun facts about me

(1) I'm a math nerd who loves spreadsheets. Give me numbers and I'll find a pattern.

(2) I live on a Costa Rica beach!

(3) I also like to exercise. Yes, I know I'm odd.

I love hearing from readers either on FB or via email (hint, hint).

Social Media Sites

Website: www.velladay.com
FB: www.facebook.com/vella.day.90
Twitter: velladay4
Gmail: velladayauthor@gmail.com

also by vella day

A WITCH'S COVE MYSTERY (Paranormal Cozy Mystery)

PINK Is The New Black (book 1)

A PINK Potion Gone Wrong (book 2)

The Mystery of the PINK Aura (book 3)

Box Set (books 1-3)

Sleuthing In The PINK (book 4)

Not in The PINK (book 5)

Gone in the PINK of an Eye (book 6)

Box Set (books 4-6)

The PINK Pumpkin Party (book 7)

Mistletoe with a PINK Bow (book 8)

The Magical PINK Pendant (book 9)

The Poisoned PINK Punch (book 10)

PINK Smoke and Mirrors (book 11)

Broomsticks and PINK Gumdrops (book 12)

Knotted Up In PINK Yarn (book 13)

Ghosts and PINK Candles (book 14)

Pilfering The PINK Pearls (book 15)

The Case of The Stolen PINK Tombstone (book 16)

The PINK Christmas Cookie Caper (book 17)

PINK Moon Rising (book 18)

A VOODOO & VAMPIRE MYSTERY (a spinoff of A Witch's

Cove Mystery)

Call Me Ghostly(Book 1)

Better Late Than Staked (Book 2)

Ghosts Just Want To Have Fun (Book 3)

SILVER LAKE SERIES (3 OF THEM)

(1). **HIDDEN REALMS OF SILVER LAKE** (Paranormal Romance)

Awakened By Flames (book 1)

Seduced By Flames (book 2)

Kissed By Flames (book 3)

Destiny In Flames (book 4)

Box Set (books 1-4)

Passionate Flames (book 5)

Ignited By Flames (book 6)

Touched By Flames (book 7)

Box Set (books 5-7)

Bound By Flames (book 8)

Fueled By Flames (book 9)

Scorched By Flames (book 10)

(2). **FOUR SISTERS OF FATE: HIDDEN REALMS OF SILVER LAKE** (Paranormal Romance)

Poppy (book 1)

Primrose (book 2)

Acacia (book 3)

Magnolia (book 4)

Box Set (books 1-4)

Jace (book 5)

Tanner (book 6)

(3). **WERES AND WITCHES OF SILVER LAKE** (Paranormal Romance)

A Magical Shift (book 1)

Catching Her Bear (book 2)

Surge of Magic (book 3)

The Bear's Forbidden Wolf (book 4)

Her Reluctant Bear (book 5)

Freeing His Tiger (book 6)

Protecting His Wolf (book 7)

Waking His Bear (book 8)

Melting Her Wolf's Heart (book 9)

Her Wolf's Guarded Heart (book 10)

His Rogue Bear (book 11)

Box Set (books 1-4)

Box Set (books 5-8)

Reawakening Their Bears (book 12)

OTHER PARANORMAL SERIES

PACK WARS (Paranormal Romance)

Training Their Mate (book 1)

Claiming Their Mate (book 2)

Rescuing Their Virgin Mate (book 3)

Box Set (books 1-3)

Loving Their Vixen Mate (book 4)

Fighting For Their Mate (book 5)

Enticing Their Mate (book 6)

Box Set (books 1-4)

Complete Box Set (books 1-6)

HIDDEN HILLS SHIFTERS (Paranormal Romance)

An Unexpected Diversion (book 1)

Bare Instincts (book 2)

Shifting Destinies (book 3)

Embracing Fate (book 4)

Promises Unbroken (book 5)

Bare 'N Dirty (book 6)

Hidden Hills Shifters Complete Box Set (books 1-6)

CONTEMPORARY SERIES

MONTANA PROMISES (Full length contemporary Romance)

Promises of Mercy (book 1)

Foundations For Three (book 2)

Montana Fire (book 3)

Montana Promises Box Set (books 1-3)

Hart To Hart (Book 4)

Burning Seduction (Book 5)

Montana Promises Complete Box Set (books 1-5)

ROCK HARD, MONTANA (contemporary romance novellas)

Montana Desire (book 1)

Awakening Passions (book 2)

PLEDGED TO PROTECT (contemporary romantic suspense)

From Panic To Passion (book 1)

From Danger To Desire (book 2)

From Terror To Temptation (book 3)

Pledged To Protect Box Set (books 1-3)

BURIED SERIES (contemporary romantic suspense)

Buried Alive (book 1)

Buried Secrets (book 2)

Buried Deep (book 3)

The Buried Series Complete Box Set (books 1-3)

A NASH MYSTERY (Contemporary Romance)

Sidearms and Silk(book 1)

Black Ops and Lingerie(book 2)

A Nash Mystery Box Set (books 1-2)

STARTER SETS (Romance)

Contemporary

Paranormal

www.ingramcontent.com/pod-product-compliance
Lightning Source LLC
LaVergne TN
LVHW090940080826
845145LV00003B/825

9781951430511